AF662522

**Hemendra Kumar Roy** (1888–1963) was a prolific writer, columnist and editor who wrote for both children and adults in Bengali. He has been credited with creating the genres of horror, speculative fiction and adventure for children in modern Bengali fiction. His characters, Bimal-Kumar (the adventurers) and Jayanta-Manik (the detectives) appeared in numerous stories and continue to be wildly popular.

Hemenbabu was also a choreographer, a competent player of the esraj who regularly performed at the Star Theatre in Calcutta and the editor of a theatre and film magazine called *Naachghar*.

**Jashodhara Chakraborti** writes, translates, teaches and speaks. She is ambidextrous, mad about music, her dog Babu and her book collection. Jashodhara lives in Calcutta, which is Kolkata if you were born in this century. She will go to ridiculous lengths for the perfect Bourbon biscuit but can be soothed in a crisis with a Kit-Kat. Or a freshly made Nolen Gur sandesh when it's winter.

As Jash Sen, she has written two young adult adventures
Find her translations at jashodharac.stck.me
Instagram: jashodharachakraborti
Facebook: Jashodhara Chakraborti
Twitter: jashodhara3

## Praise for *The Treasure of the Khasi Hills*

'A zinger of an adventure, *The Treasure of the Khasi Hills* has enough blood, ghosts, burning eyes, fisticuffs, daggers, skulls, ciphers and hidden treasure to keep the reader riveted. The style of storytelling, while perhaps unfamiliar to today's young reader, is a great illustration of how Bengali writers in the early 20th century adapted western plot styles to local stories and settings to produce highly original and entertaining works of fiction. What makes the story remarkable is that Hemen Roy's young narrator, even in the midst of his constant sense of dread, does not neglect to describe, and more importantly, delight in, the local geography—waterfalls, hills, flowers, trees, sunrises—which lends to the work a philosophical bent often missing in more recent works in the genre. A big shout-out to Jashodhara Chakraborti's excellent translation, which brings the story to seamless, throbbing life.'

—Roopa Pai

# the TREASURE of the KHASI HILLS

HEMENDRA KUMAR ROY

*Translated by* Jashodhara Chakraborti

talking CUB
An Imprint of Speaking Tiger Books

TALKING CUB
Published by Speaking Tiger Books LLP
125A, Ground Floor, Shahpur Jat,
Near Asiad Village, New Delhi - 110 049

Originally published in Bengali in 1930
This translation published by Speaking Tiger Books in 2023

Translation copyright © Jashodhara Chakraborti 2023
Introduction copyright © Jashodhara Chakraborti 2023

ISBN: 978-93-5447-510-8
eISBN: 978-93-5447-516-0

10 9 8 7 6 5 4 3 2 1

Typeset in Adobe Garamond Pro by Jojy Philip
Printed at HT Media Ltd, Greater Noida

All rights reserved.
No part of this publication may be reproduced, transmitted, or stored in a retrieval system, in any form or by any means, electronic, mechanical, photocopying, recording or otherwise, without the prior permission of the publisher.

This book is sold subject to the condition that it shall not, by way of trade or otherwise, be lent, resold, hired out, or otherwise circulated, without the publisher's prior consent, in any form of binding or cover other than that in which it is published.

*For Haha*

*Aunt*

*Teacher*

*Cheerleader in Chief*

# Contents


| | |
|---|---|
| *Introduction* | ix |
| The Skull | 1 |
| The Yaksha's Treasure | 6 |
| The Meaning of the Code | 11 |
| Ruin | 18 |
| A Plan Is Hatched | 24 |
| Burgling the Thief | 29 |
| The Black Face at the Window | 36 |
| A Silver Lining | 41 |
| Fresh Danger | 47 |
| Who Is This Thief? | 53 |
| Chhatak | 60 |
| Trouble Without Warning | 65 |

At the Khasi Hills 72

Ishaan's Story 77

Two Burning Eyes 82

The Mystery of the Pishaach 87

In the Jaws of Death 91

A Miraculous Thing 98

Trouble Among the Trees 105

Obstacle 110

Obstacle upon Obstacle 115

Supernatural 119

The Death Laugh 125

The Treasury 130

Invisible Danger 135

Ghost, Animal, or Human? 139

Karali's Other Feat 146

The Terrible Cave 152

Conclusion 157

# Introduction

Pupu was burning up
'The Treasure' turning up
Is quite the curse turned boon
For she's over the moon.
—Haha.

1978: It was peak summer. I was recovering from a bout of the measles, stick thin, as weak as a newborn and bored. Most of my days were spent in a haze of sleep or in staring at the impossibly high ceilings with its beams and rafters in our Calcutta home. On one of those dreary afternoons, my aunt, whom I call Haha (we are a family that laugh loudly and laugh a lot) returned from work and gifted me a book. It had a green and black cover and a terrified face on it. Inside, there was this little four-line verse dedicated to little Pupu a.k.a. yours truly—a pleasant little precursor to one of the best adventure stories I have ever read.

It was titled *Jawkher Dhawn*—'The Treasure of the Yaksha' and it was written by a remarkable author called Hemendra Kumar Roy or Hemen Roy. The book you hold in your hands, a translation of *Jawkher Dhawn* now called *The Treasure of the Khasi Hills*, was first published in Bengali almost a century ago in 1930. It was serialized in a Bengali magazine for children and young adults called *Mouchak*. The author was thirty-five years old at the time and well on his way to transforming books for young adults in Bengal forever.

If you were born in the Calcutta of 1930, you would find the city divided into the 'white town' where only the British and Europeans lived and the 'black town' occupied by us Indians at its northern and southern fringes. You would have come across a very different India where we Indians were second-class citizens in our own country. Your school curriculum would tell you that our civilization was primitive, rather than ancient. Stories and articles of assertion aimed to build our confidence would be looked upon with suspicion by the colonizers. Despite our revolutionaries and our push towards freedom, we were firmly under the thumb of British rule in 1930.

Into this stifling environment came Hemendra Kumar Roy's pioneering stories for children, young adults and adults. They were western in style, with detailed plots, but unabashedly nationalistic in tone and fervour. Imagine Edgar Allen Poe, Robert Louis Stevenson, Arthur Conan Doyle and H.G. Wells all rolled into one person. Imagine gun-wielding Bengali adventurers, fearless sleuths who wouldn't shy away from zombies, and scientists—then imagine one man instilling this sense of wonder and confidence among thousands of children with his pen and his imagination.

Hemen Roy opened the world of adventure, of detective fiction, of the paranormal, of fantasies, sometimes all rolled up in one breathless story for generations to come. There were stray stories of each kind before him, but Hemenbabu, as he was called, single-handedly created the genres in Bengal, especially for the younger audience. Hemen Roy wrote over eighty stories for a younger audience.

His stories embodied the new Indian youngster who embraced modernity but had no doubt in his mind that Indian nationalism and freedom were paramount. I say *his*, because, like many writers of his time and after him, the protagonists tended to be male. But if you can forgive this one shortcoming, which was a global feature of the time, you will find Hemen Roy's works fast-paced and enjoyable.

Like many a renaissance person, Hemenbabu was multifaceted. He was a famous songwriter and lyricist; had learned to appreciate art and draw under the tutelage of Abanindranath Tagore; and was the editor of the first theatre and film magazine in Bengali called *Naachghar*. He wrote songs for Manna Dey; knew a young S.D. Burman; was friends with Kazi Nazrul Islam who composed music for his songs; was a choreographer for at least one famous play; worshipped Rabindranath Tagore as his guru; and knew Saratchandra Chattopadhyay. Yet, for all his very literary friends, his own stories retained their spirit of adventure and derring-do. Hemenbabu was unique in his own right.

For those of you who like films, the old Hindi film *Bees Saal Baad* (it has mesmerizing songs that I recommend, by the way) was based on a neo-gothic story by Hemen Roy called *Nishachari Bibhishika* or 'The Horror of the Night'.

Hemen Roy was also famous for his adaptations

of famous English neo-gothic and horror stories into Bengali. They were not translations—he would completely recreate the stories in the local Bengali milieu. He was profoundly influenced by M.R. James, Sheridan Le Fanu and Mary Shelley, among others. Some of the adaptations are *Ajobe Deshe Amala* (*Alice in Wonderland*), *Haradhoner Deep* (*And Then There Were None*), and my personal favourite, *Bishalgorer Dushshashan* (*The Dushshasan of Vishalgar*)—an adaptation of Bram Stoker's *Dracula*. He also wrote historical fiction, columns and articles—although these were mainly for adults.

Hemenbabu spun at least two successful book series—Jayanta-Manik being his detective duo, Bimal-Kumar his adventure duo. He wrote around thirty Bimal-Kumar stories, some of which are also science fiction. *The Treasure of the Khasi Hills*, originally titled *Jawkher Dhon*, is the first among them. It is an adventure story featuring Bimal and Kumar, their dog Bagha who is a tough, indie dog and Bimal's faithful attendant, Ramhari. Bimal and Kumar are friends, neighbours, bachelors and fellow adventurers, although at first, Kumar is a reluctant partner.

A jawkh or yaksha is a spirit that has been a part of our mythology and folklore since time immemorial.

In mythology, yakshas are spirits with near-divine status. However, the jawkh of folklore is different. Jawkhs are created when a person is buried alive to guard a treasure forever. The uncremated, unhappy guardian of treasure has only one objective—how to escape. It is said that the jawkh or yaksha of folklore lures treasure hunters in to kill them. What does a mythical spirit like a yaksha have to do with a treasure hunt? Read on to find out.

Decades on, it is an indescribable feeling to be the translator of my favourite adventure story. Thank you, Talking Cub; my enthusiastic and encouraging editors, Sudeshna Shome Ghosh and Radhika Shenoy; and my ever-loving, talented and somewhat eccentric rock-solid family and friends for being there for me through it all. I hope I have done justice to the master storyteller. And thank you, Haha, for introducing me to the wonderful world of Hemen Roy.

Jashodhara Chakraborti
March 2023

# 1

# The Skull

When my grandfather passed, we found a small box in his iron trunk among his other belongings. My mother opened it, thinking it must contain something valuable. But all she found was an old pocketbook, and something wrapped in a dirty newspaper. She unwrapped the newspaper and immediately screamed, dropping whatever was wrapped in it.

I hurried over and asked, 'What—what happened, Ma?'

Trembling, she pointed to the floor and said, 'Kumar, throw that thing away right now!'

I looked down and saw a skull lying on the floor.

Surprised, I said, 'A skull in his iron trunk! Had Thakurda lost his mind in his old age?'

'What are you waiting for? Just throw it and sprinkle Gangajal right away!'

I chucked the skull out of the window into a dry ditch next to our house. The pocketbook I kept on a shelf. Ma put the wooden box back in the trunk.

A few days later, Karali Mukherjee from our neighborhood suddenly turned up at our house. I was very surprised to see him at our place, because I knew that my grandfather and he had not got along at all; when Thakurda was alive, I had never seen Karali Mukherjee enter our home.

Karalibabu said to me, 'Kumar, you have no elders guiding you any longer. You are still underage. All said and done, you're a boy from the neighbourhood, we should all be helping you right now. That is why I have come.'

Listening to Karalibabu's words, I thought he wasn't as bad a person as I had previously assumed. I thanked him and said, 'If I need anything, I'll come to you first thing.'

Then Karalibabu sat and talked of other things. In the course of our conversation, I said, 'Something rather interesting has been found in Thakurda's iron trunk!'

'What thing?' asked Karalibabu.

'A sandalwood box, containing a skull—'

Karalibabu's eyes suddenly burned bright like two embers. He quickly said, 'A skull?'

'Yes, and a pocketbook.'

'Where is that box now?'

'Still in the iron trunk.'

Karalibabu changed the subject after that, but I could tell that he was in the grip of some great excitement. Then he left.

That night I woke up all of a sudden. My dog, Bagha, was bringing the house down with his barking. Annoyed, I scolded him a couple of times, but all that did was cgg Bagha on further. He barked even louder than before.

Right after that, I heard the thud of footsteps. Someone had just sprinted over our terrace. Flustered, I rushed to open my bedroom door and stepped out. I looked around me, but there was no one there. I thought it was my imagination. Letting Bagha out of his leash, I returned to my room and went back to sleep.

As soon as I woke up the next morning, I heard my mother shouting her head off. I stepped outside my room and asked, 'What has happened, Ma?'

Ma said, 'Kumar, a thief tried to loot us last night!'

So, I hadn't imagined what I had heard.

'Come and take a look. He's broken open the iron trunk in the drawing room!'

Entering the drawing room, I saw she was right. The thief hadn't been able to take much though, just the sandalwood box.

But a niggling worry ate away at me. Despite all the other valuables in the trunk, why did the thief just carry that one sandalwood box? Then I remembered how excited Karalibabu had been when I had mentioned that box yesterday. Was it possible that the box was part of some sort of a mystery? Otherwise, who would carefully store a skull in a trunk?

Without alerting my mother, I rushed out. When I reached the ditch, I found the skull lying on a mound of trash! I picked it up to inspect it. The skull had been painted over on one side with some sort of dark dye, but the water in the ditch had rubbed off some of the colour. On the parts without the dye, some calculations had been carved into the bone. Burning with curiosity, I smuggled the skull back home. Some hard rubbing with soap and the dye washed off. I watched in surprise as an entire side of the skull emerged, filled with minute numbers; someone had carved them in. They looked like this:

| | | | | |
|---|---|---|---|---|
| 1 (2) 6 (3) 11 3 | 16 6 (2) | 1 14 (4) 8 (2) 11 | 15 6 14 (3) 11 (2) | 16 6 (2) |
| 12 (3) 11 (2) | 16 14 (2)(2) | 4 14 (4) 10 | 16 6 (2) | 16 14 (5) 11 8 |
| 1 (1) 15 (2) | 16 (2) 11 | 20 (1) 14 3 15 | (2) (1) 15 16 | 15 16 (4) 12 |
| 5 (4) | 14 (3) 5 6 16 | (2) (3) 5 6 16 | 20 (1) 14 3 15 | 1 (5) 3 3 6 (1) |
| (3) 11 | 16 6 (2) | (2) (1) 15 16 | 16 (4) | 16 6 (2) |
| 9 (2) 4 16 | 15 (3) 19 | 20 (1) 14 3 15 | (1) 6 (2) (1) 3 | 16 6 14 (2) (2) |
| 14 (4) 2 8 15 | 3 (3) 5 | (5) 11 3 (2) 14 | 4 (4) 14 | 15 (2) 17 (2) 11 |
| 2 (5) 1 (3) 16 15 | (1) 11 3 | 4 (3) 11 3 | 20(4)(5)14 | 12 (1) 16 6 |

# 2

# The Yaksha's Treasure

What could be the meaning of these strange numbers? I obsessed about them, but couldn't make head or tail of the whole thing.

Then I remembered my grandfather's pocketbook. It was kept with the skull—might I get an answer to this mystery in its pages?

I immediately pulled it out from the shelf. On opening it, I found it filled with writing from cover to cover. I read the first sixteen or seventeen pages, but it was all inconsequential drivel. Then suddenly, somewhere, I saw:

*September, 1904. We were coming through a forest one*

*evening on our way back from Assam. It was nearly dusk, we were descending from a hill to the valley below. All of a sudden, we saw an enormous tiger some distance away. It was crouching—about to pounce on someone! Then I saw a hermit some distance away beside the track, lying down under a tree. It was him the tiger was aiming at!*

*I shouted out right away. The porters shouted along with me. The hermit woke up and the tiger, startled by the din, saw us and disappeared in one jump.*

*The hermit had understood all. He came to me and expressed his gratitude, saying, 'Son, today you saved me from the jaws of a tiger.'*

*I said, 'Thakur, is it sensible to sleep in the middle of the jungle like this?'*

*The hermit said, 'This jungle is my home, son.'*

*I said, 'But you could have lost your life just now!'*

*He said, 'Where, son? I didn't lose it after all. God sent you to me at just the right time.'*

*I learnt he was headed the same way as us. So we took the hermit along with us and moved on.*

*The hermit stayed with us for two days. I took care of him to the best of my ability, leaving no stone unturned. Before taking our leave on the third day, he told me, 'Son, I am truly pleased by your unstinted service. You saved my life as well. Before I leave, I want to give you some directions.'*

*I asked, 'Directions to what, thakur?'*

*He replied, 'To a yaksha's treasure.'*

*I asked eagerly, 'Yaksha's treasure? Where is it, thakur?'*

*'In the Khasia* hills.'*

*I said in dismay, 'But how will I know where it is, thakur?'*

*He said, 'I'll tell you. Have you heard of the Roopnath caves in the Khasi hills?'*

*'Yes, I have. Legend has it that one can go all the way to China from these caves, and that many years ago, a Chinese emperor had come through these caves with his troops to attack India.'*

*The hermit said, 'Indeed. If you go about sixty miles to the west, you will find an ancient temple in the middle of the valley. The temple is in ruins, some years down the line there will probably be no signs left of it. Once there was a sprawling monastery there for Buddhist monks. A king from those times hid all his wealth in this monastery before embarking on a battle*

---

* The old Bengali name for Khasi hills. I have taken the liberty of using Khasi hills throughout from now on.

*with a foreign enemy. But he lost the battle. Afraid that his wealth would fall into the hands of the enemy, the king hid it all in one place and left a yaksha to guard his treasure for him. Then he escaped, but he never returned. The treasure is still in the same place.' Then he gave me the directions to the monastery in detail.*

*I said, 'But what if someone has already found out about the treasure?'*

*The hermit said, 'No one has. It is very difficult terrain, no one knows that there is a monastery there, no one goes there. Even if they reach the monastery and look for it for the rest of their lives, they won't find it.' Saying this, the hermit fished out a skull from his sack.*

*I asked him in surprise, 'What's that for, thakur?'*

*The hermit said, 'This is the skull of the yaksha who is guarding the treasure. I have put a spell on it. The yaksha will not harm the person who carries it. These numbers and calculations carved on the skull are in a code. I will also give you the key to the code, and with its help, you will know exactly where to find the treasure.' Saying this, the hermit explained the secret key to the code to me.*

*I contemplated this for an entire year; but wasn't confident enough to venture into that difficult terrain on my own. Finally I decided to trust my neighbour,*

*Karali, and told him everything, adding, 'Karali, you're a young man, if you come with me, I'll give you an equal share.'*

*But I hadn't realized that Karali would betray me. He kept trying to dupe me of the skull. He also sent mercenary thieves to try and steal it, but failed. Thank heavens I had not told him the whereabouts of the yaksha's treasure.*

*But I have given up all hope of going to the Khasi hills. Why should I risk losing my life on alien soil in my old age to wild bears or tigers or bandits? And I no longer trust anyone enough to take them with me—who knows, a friend could kill me in the end for greed!*

*Still, I have written down everything in this pocketbook. It might come in useful to my descendants in the future. But if any of my kin truly decide to travel to that Buddhist monastery, they must think of the dangers that will befall them before they embark. Danger will follow this mission every step of the way.*

I sat with the pocketbook in my hand, transfixed.

## 3

# The Meaning of the Code

Karalibabu's such a dangerous man! He had tried to trick Thakurda, but hadn't managed it. But he still hadn't given up hope in all these years. I now realized that Karalibabu had landed up at home just to learn where the skull was kept. The thief had come at night with the sole objective of stealing the skull, there was no doubt about it. Thank goodness I had chucked it into the ditch next to our house!

What was I supposed to do now, though? The key to the treasure was right here on this skull, but I couldn't make head or tail of it even after going over it many times. I flipped through every page of the pocketbook, but Thakurda had left no clues there either. I was very annoyed with Thakurda. There was no way to understand the actual message.

Then I thought, what would have been the point of understanding the message anyway? I was seventeen years old. Studying in my second year. Had never stepped outside Calcutta in my life. And there were the Khasi Hills, who knows in what corner and somewhere in them the 'Roopnath caves'—just finding out all of this would be impossible for me! To top it all, that dense forest, where wild animals roam freely in broad daylight! And finally some Buddhist monastery where there is a yaksha's treasure—yet another spooky thing! What if I lost my life, like Alibaba's brother Qasim, in my lust for wealth? Just thinking about all this made my heart flutter.

Then all of a sudden, I thought of Bimal. He was my dear friend, and from our neighborhood as well. He's three odd years older than me, appearing for his B.A. this year. I haven't met a cleverer person than Bimal. And he's as strong as an ox, he wrestled every day and did three hundred bench presses daily. To top it all, he had travelled widely even at his young age—why, just last year he had been to Assam. I've never hidden anything from Bimal. Whether I go or not, I decided, let me just show Bimal the skull once.

That afternoon when I landed up at Bimal's place, he was sitting and cleaning his gun. Seeing me, he said, 'Kumar! What brings you here?'

I said, 'A puzzle has put me in a complete spot, my friend.'

Bimal said, 'Which puzzle?'

I took out the skull and said, 'This one.'

Bimal stared at the skull for a while in surprise. Then he asked, 'What's this?'

I pushed the pocketbook towards him and said, 'My grandfather's pocketbook. Read it and you'll understand everything.'

'Fine, hang on. Let me quickly finish cleaning the gun. I'd gone hunting for birds yesterday. The gun's collected a lot of dirt.'

Having cleaned the gun, Bimal washed his hands and said, 'What's the matter, Kumar? Are you interning with some tantric? Why do you have a skull in your hand?'

'Why don't you read the pocketbook first?' I asked in return.

'Fine,' said Bimal and started reading. After a while

I saw his expression change from one of resignation to wonder and curiosity.

As soon as he finished reading, Bimal quickly picked up the skull and scrutinized it, turning it over several times. Then he sighed and said, 'How astonishing!'

'Could you make any sense of the sums?'

'No,' he said.

'Neither could I.'

'But I'm not letting go this easily. You go home now, Kumar. Leave the skull with me for now. I am determined to learn its secret! Come back tomorrow morning.'

'But be careful,' I said.

'Why?'

'Because Karali Mukherjee had sent a man to steal the skull from me last night.'

'Karali? None of his henchmen will have the guts to stick their necks in my home,' Bimal said.

'I know that. Still, it never hurts to be careful.' And I came back home.

I rushed to Bimal's place as soon as it was light the next day. His door was always open for me. I went straight to his study and found him poring over his table, writing something, with the skull in front of him. At the sound of my footsteps, he quickly picked up the skull in an effort to hide it. Upon realizing it was me, he said, 'Oh, it's you! I thought it was someone else.'

'You were full of bravado yesterday, so why are you so scared this morning?'

'Yesterday? Yesterday I hadn't figured all the details out. I have realized that we have to do everything with the utmost caution from now on. No one can know anything about this.'

'Could you understand the calculations?'

'Everything that needed to be understood, yes.'

I jumped up in joy, shouting, 'You understood everything? Really?'

Bimal said, 'Hush! Don't shout! You never know who might overhear. Calm down and take a seat.'

I pulled up a chair and said, 'Tell me what's written in the skull.'

Bimal said slowly, 'I couldn't make out anything at first. When I'd nearly lost all hope after trying for four hours, I suddenly recalled something. Quite a while ago, I had read a book in English which had explained many ciphers and codes at length. This book mentioned that thieves and robbers in Europe often use a cipher not very different from this one.

They allocate a number to every alphabet, so "A" is 1, "B" is 2, "C" is 3, etcetera. I thought perhaps this skull employs something similar as its code. On trying, I found that my surmise was correct. Then I deciphered these symbols very easily.'

I asked eagerly, 'So what could you make out after reading it?'

Bimal extended a sheet of paper towards me, saying, 'The symbols on the skull are divided into forty cells. I've arranged them in exactly the same way.'

The sheet had the following words:

| behind | the | broken | shrine | the |
|---|---|---|---|---|
| pine | tree | from | the | trunk |
| base | ten | yards | east | stop |
| go | right | eight | yards | buddha |
| in | the | east | to | the |
| left | six | yards | ahead | three |
| rocks | dig | under | for | seven |
| cubits | and | find | your | path |

I read the sheet, thinking how marvellously clever Bimal was.

'Let me explain the code to you,' Bimal said. 'The script is divided into vowels and consonants. The vowels are given numbers from 1 to 5. So "A" is 1, "E" is 2 and so on. The consonants have likewise been given numbers as well. Here, "B" is 1, "C" is 2, "D" is 3, etcetera.

'When a word has a vowel, it appears next to the consonant in brackets. So 1(2) stands for "be" and 6(3) stands for "hi". When a word starts with a vowel, it appears on its own. So (3) stands for "i" and 10 under it stands for the consonant "n"—"in".'

I picked up the skull to inspect it once more, but it accidentally fell on the marble floor with a loud crash. Picking it up immediately, I scanned it once and said, 'Oh no! A bit of the skull's nicked.'

Bimal asked, 'Which bit?'

'The first seven cells…behind the broken shrine the sal tree—that bit.'

Bimal said, 'Had this happened earlier, it would have ruined everything. But there's nothing to fear now. I've copied the symbols on to a piece of paper. But we have to be very careful. It is best to keep the calculations and destroy the words now.' Saying this, he tore the sheet of paper into shreds.

When required, we would be able to solve the code in five minutes, but no one other than us would be able to get at the message from the symbols on the skull.

# 4

# Ruin

'But Bimal, now that we know the meaning of the code, what shall we do?' I asked.

Bimal interrupted me and said, 'There are no buts here, Kumar. We *have* to go! Such a strange affair! I won't be satisfied until I see this through to the end.'

'Who'll come along with us?'

'No one. Just you and I.'

'But it's a very inaccessible place. Should we go without a team?'

'It's not inaccessible at all. I know the way very well. I can take you up to Roopnath caves myself. I don't know the way from there of course, or how the path is, but it won't take us long to find out. Are you afraid of danger? Don't be. Don't fear danger. Humanity wouldn't have reached where it is today had it feared danger. Even a child can take the easy path, where's the credit in that? But a man among men allows danger to temper him with a smile and emerges truer.'

I said, 'But how will humanity gain if we lose our lives to pigheadedness? I'm not a coward—of course I'm ready to go wherever you say. But we shouldn't do anything blindly. You know how the proverb says, "Look before you leap".'

Bimal said, 'I've thought through everything there is to think of, no more thinking now.'

'When do you want to go?'

'I'm ready. Tomorrow, the day after, whenever you say.'

'So soon! We have to organize ourselves before we leave!'

'Organize my foot. We're not going there to set up home. It's best to travel light when it comes to jobs like these. Two odd bags and the two of us—that's it.'

'Which route will you take?'

Bimal said, 'We have to cross Kamrup and then climb the Khasi hills. Right next to the Khasi hills, like a twin, there's another called Jayanti. To the north of these lie Kamrup and Nabagram. To the east lie North Kachar, the Naga hills and the Kopili river. To the south lies Srihatta and to the west, the Garo hills.'*

'Are the Khasi hills very high?'

'Uh-huh. Four thousand in some places, five thousand in others and nearly six and a half thousand feet high sometimes. There are many waterfalls in these hills. Among these the Mawsmai falls near Cherrapunji and Beadon falls near Shillong are the large ones. The first one is one thousand, eight hundred feet high, the second one is six hundred feet high. Mawsmai is the second highest waterfall in the world. There are hot springs in the hills too. The Khasi hills have two seasons, monsoon and winter. Rain and thunderstorms are common. March and April arc a bit dry, so one gets a touch of spring. Cherrapunji in the Khasi hills is famous for its rainfall.'

'Are there tigers there?' I asked.

---

* Jayanti, Nabagram, North Kachar and Srihatta are the old Bengali names for Jayantia hills, Nagaon, North Cachar and Sylhet respectively.

Bimal laughed. 'Why just tigers? The jungles there have them all—elephants, rhinos, wild buffaloes, wild boar. But hardly any snakes.'

I scratched my head and said, 'Hmm, there is that.'

Bimal slapped my back and said, 'Kumar, you think the jungles are more dangerous than they actually are because you've never stepped out of Calcutta. And I'll be there with you, so what do you need to be afraid of? You know I have experience of big game hunting, even at this age. I hold two licenses to use guns. I'll give you one. You've not hunted any game yet, but I taught you how to shoot ages ago, this will be a good test of your skill.'

I didn't say anything further and returned to my place. I was scared, but I was also excited. I had always wanted to see new places. When I read about remote places in books, my heart would grow wings and fly off there. Sometimes I wished to build a hut with my own hands on a desolate island like Robinson Crusoe and live there for days on end, sometimes I wanted to be Sindbad the sailor and fly to the skies with a Roc bird, cook on the back of a whale and serve the old man on the island his just desserts. At other times I wanted to delve into the depths of the ocean in a submarine and loot all the treasures of Pataal! I cannot tell you how many of these dreams I have dreamed. You will laugh at me if you hear them all.

The truth is, more than the yaksha's treasure, the thrill of seeing a new place cheered me up considerably. All my worries and fears faded away.

As soon as I was near my home, my dog Bagha greeted me with six inches of hanging tongue and a wagging tail.

I said, 'So Bagha, want to come along to the Khasi hills with us?'

It looked like Bagha understood what I said. He stood on his hind legs and wrapped my waist with his front ones, then proceeded to lick my face with great enthusiasm. I quickly moved my face and extricated myself.

My Bagha isn't some foreign pedigree dog, he is a local mongrel, but you wouldn't know that by looking at him. Bagha is living proof of the fact that with proper care, our local dogs can look just as impressive as the pedigreed ones. He is huge, yellow-brown with black spots on his coat, a bit like a leopard, which is why I call him Bagha. He doesn't know the meaning of fear and is very strong. Once a huge hound of some sort had chased him, but one bite from Bagha and that hound had nearly died. I decided we'd take him along with us.

Early next morning, someone woke me up with a great deal of urgency. I opened my eyes and saw Bimal by my bed. He was panting.

Surprised, I sat up and said, 'How come you're here so early in the morning?'

Bimal, still panting, said, 'We're ruined!'

'Ruined! Why?'

'The skull was stolen from my home last night,' Bimal said.

'What!' I exclaimed, dumbstruck and at my wits' end.

# 5

# A Plan Is Hatched

'How did the skull get stolen, Bimal?' I asked.

'Don't know. I woke up in the morning to find my study door open, someone had broken into the room last night! My heart immediately missed a beat. I had kept the skull in my table drawer and locked it. I ran in to see that the drawer was pulled wide and that the skull was not in it!'

I exclaimed, 'This must be Karali Mukherjee's handiwork. It is he who's sent goons to steal the skull. But what surprises me is how Karali Mukherjee knew the skull was at your place.'

Bimal said, 'Karali must have stationed spies

everywhere. He knows all about what we're planning and what we're doing.'

'But what will he achieve with just the skull? He doesn't know the coded message after all.'

Bimal said, 'Kumar, never underestimate the enemy. If we could understand the message, then why can't Karali crack it as well with just a bit of effort?'

'But all of the message is not on the skull anymore! It fell from my hand yesterday and got nicked. Remember?'

Bimal absently said, 'Still, one can't be complacent,' while thinking of something.

All of a sudden, I remembered something else. I hurriedly asked him, 'Is Thakurda's pocketbook stolen as well?'

Bimal said, 'No, that is one saving grace. I had taken the pocketbook to bed with me last night to read it once again, properly. Before I went to sleep, I put it under my pillow, so the thief couldn't take it.'

Somewhat relieved, I said, 'Well, we're still safe, my friend. The actual address to the treasure is in that pocketbook. Without the address, Karali can't do anything even if he can work out the message! But be very careful, Bimal! The pocketbook shouldn't get stolen now.'

Bimal said, 'I'll arrange for that today itself. Wherever the pocketbook mentions the route and the address, I shall blot it out in such a way that no one can read it.'

I said, 'But then, we'll be in trouble as well!'

Bimal laughed and said, 'Never fear. I'll copy down the route and the address on a fresh sheet of paper in code. No one has the key to that code other than me.'

After a pause, I asked, 'What shall we do now?'

Bimal said, 'First we have to retrieve the skull.'

Surprised, I asked, 'How to do that?'

'Just how he took the skull from us!'

'Burgle the thief?'

Bimal said, 'What other way is there? I'll break into Karali's house somehow this very night. You'll come along as well.'

A bit nervous, I said, 'But if Karali finds out, he'll get *us* arrested for stealing! There is no proof that he has stolen the skull from us, after all.'

'We have to do what destiny has in store for us. But it is true that Karali cannot catch either of us while I'm alive,' Bimal was sounding desperate.

Unable to convince myself, I said, 'No, Bimal, let's avoid breaking into his house. We can't have a scandal in the neighbourhood.'

Bimal flew into a rage at this. 'Damn it, you coward, you're planning to go to Roopnath caves with *this* brand of courage? Why don't you just be the mollycoddled little boy and sit on your mother's lap at home—I'll return your pocketbook right away,' saying this he briskly strode towards the door.

I quickly brought him back and said, 'Bimal, you've misunderstood, I am not scared at all. I was just saying—'

Bimal interrupted me and said, 'I don't want to listen to what you're saying. Tell me clearly, are you ready to come with me to Karali's place tonight or not?'

'I'm ready.'

Gladdened, Bimal shook both my hands in a mighty handshake and said, 'Hmm, there speaks a good boy. If you want to be man, be a daredevil first.'

I laughed. 'Daredevils get strung up, though.'

Bimal said, 'No one who lies in bed cheats death either. If we have to die anyway, it's much better to die like a warrior than die lying in bed! All these good boys you all approve of—I can't stand those whimpering lumps of lard. They are the ones terrified of the British, they are the ones who can't survive danger, they die—but like cowards. They are the bane of the Bengalis. The races who are living with their head held high in today's world have all disregarded Death and aimed to be the best. Do you understand, Kumar? Danger makes me happy.'

# 6

# Burgling the Thief

It was a moonless night. The darkness seemed to coalesce around us. Only the fireflies occasionally blinked everywhere—just like the thousand eyes of the demon of the dark.

Our house is in the outskirts of Calcutta, the neighborhood isn't as dense as the rest of the city yet. The houses are all far apart—there are more trees than residents. In other words, we live in Calcutta only by name, this place cannot quite be called Calcutta yet.

Right next to our house is an open grassland and in that grassland Bimal and I sat hidden in a large taro bush, waiting for the right moment. Karali

Mukherjee's house was on the other side of the grassland.

Sensing our presence, the mosquitoes around us were buzzing around happily in anticipation of a free meal. Every mosquito in the vicinity had turned up on hearing this band and were lovingly caressing us with their collective proboscis. Unable to take this terrible caress any more, I whispered to Bimal, 'Hey—this can't be borne for much longer!'

Bimal only said, 'Be still!'

'Can't you comprehend how difficult it is to do that?'

'Of course, I do! How do you think *I'm* keeping still?'

I couldn't argue with that. So I kept still.

By the time there were swollen blotches all over my face and limbs, it was the dead of night; the church clock loudly tolled one o'clock, making my heart thump.

Bimal stood up and said, 'Now it's time!'

I was ready anyway. I leaped out of the bushes.

Bimal said, 'First, put this mask on!'

Bimal had bought two expensive imported masks from Radhabazar this afternoon. Both were terrifying—guaranteed to scare the living daylights out of anyone who suddenly saw them in the dead of night. The idea behind wearing these was that no one would recognize us even if they saw us.

We put on the masks and walked towards Karali's house in silence. Once we reached the rear, Bimal said, 'Tuck your dhoti pleats into your back.'

I said, 'But there's no back door here!'

Bimal said, 'Who's using the door? Have we been invited to dinner? There's a big banyan tree here. One of its branches falls directly on to Karali's terrace. We'll use the branch to gain entry!' Bimal raised the darkened lantern in his hand and a thin beam of light fell on the branch.

I wasn't too happy with how we were going to enter, but I said nothing and climbed the banyan tree along with Bimal.

Once we'd climbed a fair height, Bimal said, 'Now—very carefully—come along here! Look—that's the branch—we have to climb this branch and jump on to the roof.'

I saw the vague outline of the branch in the darkness. Bimal moved along the branch first. A slight thud told me he had landed on the roof.

I held on to the branch with both arms and legs and inched ahead, fearing I'd fall at any moment.

Not even the goddess of healing would be able to save me if I fell from that height.

Without warning, Bimal's muffled voice said, 'That's it! Now swing from the branch.'

My heart in my mouth, I held on to the branch with both arms and swung.

'Now let go!'

As soon as I let go of the branch, I landed with a soft thud on the terrace. Bimal slapped my back and said, 'Well done!'

But I was just not easy in my mind. We'd entered someone else's house like thieves and were sure to be handcuffed like thieves if we were caught. Then there was the other worry: how shall we escape? We had entered by leaping on to the terrace, but we couldn't very well leap up to that high branch to leave. I shared my concerns with Bimal.

Bimal said, 'We had to enter via the tree because the front door is shut from the inside. When we escape, we'll just leave through the front door.'

'But the house has a guard!'

'We'll fix him when the time comes. Now, let's check out where the stairs are. Remember to tiptoe.'

We found the stairs at the west corner of the terrace. Bimal led the way down, I followed behind.

There was a room immediately after the stairs ended. Bimal put his ear on the door and told me in a quiet voice, 'Someone's sleeping in this room. And snoring.'

We made our way to the main corridor using the darkened lantern's narrow beam to guide us. Three rooms on one side—all shut from the inside. Bimal stood in silence and considered the situation. As for myself, I lost all hope. Such a huge mansion. We knew nothing of the layout inside. Somewhere in this maze lay hidden a small skull. How on earth were we supposed to sniff it out? Bimal was being foolhardy. All this hassle. It was going to be for nothing!

All at once, Bimal said, 'There's a bit of light visible through one of the doors on the other side of the corridor. Let's go there.'

Bimal tiptoed over to that door. It gave way at the slightest push. Bimal peeped through the gap for a while, then turned to whisper into my ear, 'Look!'

What I saw through the gap in the door made my heart dance with joy! Karali, snoring with his head resting on the table, and close to his head—what we'd come looking for—the skull! Karali had probably been trying to understand the cipher, and must have nodded off, exhausted. So he really was the thief!

Very gingerly, Bimal opened the door a little wider and tiptoed into the room. Standing behind a sleeping Karali, he picked up the skull from the table. Then, grinning, he stepped out of the room. I had never imagined that we'd succeed so easily.

Now for the escape. Once we were outside, we would be free!

We climbed down to the ground floor. The front door was just across the courtyard. But here's the rub: the beam of the lantern showed a burly man spreadeagled in blissful sleep right in front of the front door.

However, Bimal didn't hesitate for a moment. He just stepped over the guard very softly and started unbolting the front door. My heart thumped in fear against my chest. The slightest sound and we were ruined.

Bimal was such a hero! He opened the door carefully without a single sound. But a bug played spoilsport. It suddenly rushed into my nose and I let out a great big sneeze right away.

The guard woke up! He let out a terrific roar. 'Who's there?'

The lantern was in my hand at the time. In its light I saw Bimal turn around at lightning speed, then leap on the guard like a tiger, holding his neck in a death grip. The guard let out a few moans and soon fell in a dead faint.

What's left to say? We ran for our lives! No racehorse could have caught up with us then. We sprinted back home in one stretch and then breathed again freely.

# 7

# The Black Face at the Window

We drank a glass of cold water each and sat in the living room. It was two thirty at night.

'No sleeping tonight. We're leaving for Assam by tomorrow afternoon's train.' Bimal said.

Surprised, I said, 'What! So soon?'

'It won't do to delay. Karali rascal now holds a grudge against us. He must have realized by now that only we could have stolen the skull from him. Who knows what trouble he might create? We have to say our farewells and leave tomorrow itself.'

I objected. 'Ma has gone to Shantipur, to my uncle's. How can I leave without letting her know?'

'Send her a letter. Tell her you're off on a sightseeing trip to Assam, but you couldn't meet her because the plan was made at such short notice.'

I wasn't convinced. 'Fine, I'll write the letter, but we're going on such a big mission, there's a lot to prepare. Will I be able to organize everything by tomorrow afternoon?'

Bimal said testily, 'You don't have to do anything special. I'll do all the organizing that needs to be done. You just carry clothes and a couple of sets of coats and trousers, all right, my worthless genius?'

'Why? What do we need coats and trousers for?'

'We're going to jungles and hills. Fussing with your dhoti like a dapper gentleman from the city will not do there. You'll be in constant trouble then.'

I pondered this in silence.

Bimal said, 'I had thought that just the two of us would go. But looking at how immature you are, I'm thinking it would be better to take one more person along.'

'Who'll you take?'

'My manservant Ramhari. He's an old family retainer; trustworthy, intelligent and very strong. He can give his life for me with a smile.'

'Not a bad idea. Then I'll also take Bagha with me. I hope you don't mind—'

'Hush!' said Bimal and stood up with one swift movement. Then he suddenly ran to one of the windows and pushed it wide open. I clearly saw a grotesque black face move to one side at lightning speed. Someone must have been eavesdropping on us. Bimal didn't pause either, he picked up a man-high thick bamboo stick from one corner of the room and ran out. I bolted the door and sat down stiffly!

After a while, Bimal returned and called me from outside. I opened the door and asked him hurriedly, 'Could you catch him?'

Still panting, Bimal returned the stick to its old place and said, 'No, I chased him for a long distance, but couldn't catch him!'

'Who do you think the man was?'

'Who else? One of Karali's men. Most likely a hired goon. Kumar, do you realize the seriousness of the situation? That man's probably heard every word of what we've said!'

'Bimal, you're right. We shouldn't delay any longer. We have to leave tomorrow.'

'That we will, but it is very likely that danger will accompany us.'

'Meaning?'

'Meaning Karali will probably travel with us, along with his retinue.'

I was totally discouraged at this. Bimal, too, sat and thought hard. After a long time, he said, 'Whatever happens will happen. But curling up in our rooms like a pair of earthworms for fear of Karali Mukherjee—that is *not* going to happen. It's settled, we're leaving tomorrow itself.'

I pleaded, 'Bimal, don't be pigheaded.'

Bimal punched the stool and said, 'I will go, come what may. If you are afraid, stay at home. I'll get the yaksha's treasure and deliver it to you personally. Let's see who loses—Karali or me.'

I held his hand and said, 'Bimal, I am not afraid. I'll definitely come along if you're going. But just think through this, it could culminate in bloodshed in the middle of the jungle. Karali has many more people. We won't be able to do anything.'

Bimal smiled in derision and said, 'To hell with Karali. Kumar, I am not just strong, I also have some strength up here in my brains. You don't worry about a thing, come along with me and watch me lead him a merry dance.'

I know Bimal very well. He doesn't know what

idle boasting is. If he's reassuring me, he must have thought up a new plan. Therefore, free of worry, I said, 'Fine, my friend, I'm okay with whatever you say.'

# 8

# A Silver Lining

We packed all night, getting an hour's sleep just before dawn, then left home on time for the train. Our group consisted of Bimal's trusty manservant Ramhari and my dog Bagha. Two big bags, a suitcase and an Icmic[*] cooker—Bimal didn't allow us to carry anything other than these.

But the bags held everything we could possibly need: knives, scissors, a first-aid kit, a camera, an electric torch, a flask, biscuits, fruits and cans of

[*] An Icmic cooker was a precursor to the rice cooker. It had four compartments and steam cooked food over a coal fire. It was extremely popular in Bengali homes at the turn of the century.

potted meat and fish, some books on Assam in English, exercise books, two small cushions, rugs and the two masks. Bimal felt we might need them later as well. Other than these, the bags held a multitude of other knickknacks that I couldn't identify. The suitcase held our clothes. Each of us carried a thick stick, ones that could split open a man's head, if need be. Needless to say, Bimal didn't forget his two guns.

I felt strangely melancholic as I left home. I was leaving for who knows which foreign place,* where tigers and wild animals and enemies might lie in wait. I hadn't even touched Ma's feet before I left—who knows if I'll ever return and see her in this lifetime! At one time I thought I'd tell Bimal, 'I won't go!' but I steeled myself instead, because I didn't want him to think of me as a coward.

I think Bimal took a look at my face and understood what I was going through, for he suddenly asked me, 'Kumar, are you feeling sad?'

I told the truth. 'A little, of course.'

'For your mother?'

'Yes.'

---

* People travelled very little in those days. The railways were new and Assam was considered 'foreign' by the people of Bengal.

'Don't worry. There is a high probability that you'll meet your mother this very evening.'

Taken aback, I asked, 'How's that? We're off to Assam.'

'That's true, we are,' said Bimal and looked all around him with an anxious expression on his face. He must have been checking for any enemies who might be following us. But no one could be seen.

Bimal's car was waiting to take us to the station. It set off once we had all boarded. Bimal was lost in his thoughts for the entire journey, only breaking his reverie to look outside the window to check if we were being followed.

We alighted from the car at Sealdah station. I looked around carefully once and said, 'Bimal, there's nothing to fear for now. Karali's men have not been able to follow us.'

Not replying to this, Bimal said, 'You all wait here. I'll buy the tickets.'

Once he returned with the tickets, Bimal entered the station with us. He took Bagha to the animal compartment. Bagha didn't want to leave me at all, finally Bimal had to drag him by the leash and put him in there.

There was still some time left for the train to

leave. Seeing the humid heat in the compartment, I stepped down on to the platform for some air. Strolling, I reached right at the end of the train. My gaze skimmed over a coach. I had goose pimples all over. Karali was sitting inside the compartment! Two goons were sitting with him. They were engrossed in a conversation and gesturing wildly. They couldn't see me. I quickly boarded my compartment, after running back as fast as I could.

Bimal saw me and said, 'What's the matter, Kumar? Why are you running with your eyes bulging out of your head?'

'Disaster!'

Bimal smiled. 'You've seen Karali, haven't you? So what? That's hardly a disaster. I knew he wouldn't let go of us. Anyway, you just relax and sit down. Don't be afraid.'

I couldn't dismiss the whole thing as lightly as Bimal. I sat down on my seat quietly enough, but I felt really low. Bimal saw my body language and simply smiled. The train started.

Who knew what lay in store for us? It looked very likely that we would meet with an untimely death in the jungles finally. Who knew how many men Karali had with him? He won't stop following us now that he's come prepared like this. I thought of this and other myriad troubles, real and imagined, and shuddered.

But Bimal, unperturbed, rested his feet on the seat opposite and started reading a book.

The train stopped at a station. Bimal stuck his head out of the window to check and said, 'Kumar, get ready! The next station's Ranaghat. We're getting off there.'

What new madness was this? 'We're getting off at Ranaghat? Why?'

'From there to Shantipur, to your uncle's place. We're going to meet your mother.'

'Why did you change your mind all of a sudden?'

'I haven't changed my mind, I just didn't tell you. I had planned all this yesterday. Here, look, the tickets are for Shantipur. Do you understand why?'

'No.'

'I knew perfectly well that Karali would follow us since his spy had heard us say yesterday that we were bound for Assam. Even now, he thinks we are going to Assam and nowhere else. Let him assume that and sit tight in his compartment, while we alight at Ranaghat. We'll stay at your uncle's place for a few days, enjoy ourselves, whereas Karali will be completely lost once he learns we are not on the train. He'll definitely think we've taken an alternate route. He will lose heart and return to Calcutta, whereas we will take your mother's blessings and set out for Assam after a few days without anyone the wiser.'

Finally, some good news. Karali tricked and a meeting with my mother, just as I had wished for—killing two birds with one stone, indeed! I shook Bimal delightedly by the hand and said, 'You are just so clever! I am completely in awe of your intelligence.'

As soon as the train reached Ranaghat, we got off. No one spotted us.

# 9

# Fresh Danger

We bade farewell to my mother after three days of being treated like princes. Ma didn't want to let go of us that easily, though. I hadn't mentioned the yaksha's treasure or any of the associated risks. All she knew was that we were off sightseeing in Assam.

When we were leaving, she called Bimal and said, 'I am entrusting the last lamp of this clan to you, son. Look after him.'

Bimal said, 'There's nothing to fear, Ma. He's no longer a little boy, you don't have to worry about him anymore.'

'Still, son, don't you leave Kumar alone anywhere. He's very headstrong. There's no saying what he might do. He's not as calm and prudent as you are. If he were, I wouldn't have to worry at all.'

Bimal smiled a little and said, 'Fine, Ma. I'll be with him, and I'll watch him for any headstrong behaviour.'

I laughed inside. If only Ma had a whiff of who was the actual headstrong one!

Taking Ma's blessings, Bimal, Ramhari and I set out, with Bagha following us. But as soon as he saw the train waiting at Shantipur station, Bagha tucked his tail between his legs and looked utterly forlorn. He knew he would now be taken away and made to stay alone in the animal compartment.

We got into our actual train once we alighted at Ranaghat. Bimal said happily, 'Well! No more worries about Karali this time round. He's probably sitting in Assam, wringing his hands in despair, cursing us.'

I said, 'He may have returned to Calcutta.'

'Why Calcutta? I have no problems even if he's gone to Hell,' said Bimal and laughed. 'Come, let's board the train.'

The train stopped at Sara Ghat* very late in the

---

* Sara Ghat is in Rajshahi, western Bangladesh, on the banks of the Padma river.

night. I'm talking of the time when the famous Sara bridge over the Padma had not yet been built. In those days, everyone had to detrain at Sara Ghat and take the steamer across the Padma and board another train on the other side. So we had to collect all our stuff and Bagha and alight once we were at Sara.

As I've mentioned before, I'd never stepped outside Calcutta before. Just looking at the scenic beauty around me while on the steamer was magical. On seeing the Padma, I realized for the first time that there could be a broader river than the Ganga in Calcutta. There was a moon in the sky and the Padma swayed and danced at a great speed, bathed in the moonlight, its waves made of watered silver. Banks of white sand rose and disappeared in the middle of the river at times like landscapes in a dream. Fairies must have been playing on this silent sandbank till a moment ago. They must have just hidden, terrified at the roar of the steamer—thinking it was some demon—and disappeared into thin air.

The steamer raced towards the other side, avoiding the sandbank. The khalasis, the dockworkers, judging the depth of the river yelled out instructions to no one in particular. On one end of the steamer a mixed group of men and women sat huddled together, or stood in a crowd creating a commotion. On the upper decks, white men and women sat under dazzling lights for dinner, resplendent. But as I turned my head to the other side, I found myself at the end of a man's sharp, sidelong glance. As soon as our eyes met, he walked away at great speed and disappeared into the crowd.

The steamer banked; we embarked and headed towards the station. The monstrous Assam Mail was waiting for us, bellowing smoke; we ensconced ourselves in its belly.

I had the window seat. There was another train on the other side of the platform, crowded with passengers to Darjeeling. White ladies and gentlemen were making their beds in the first- and second-class compartments so they could sleep through the night's journey. Seeing their preparations, my eyelids felt heavy with sleep. I was trying to lie down and turn in for the night, when I saw the man from the steamer standing on the platform and watching us with that same look.

This time I got suspicious. I turned to Bimal and said, 'Hey, look, look!'

Bimal replied while placing his blanket over his

bench, 'No more looking. Now is the time to get some shuteye.'

'No, no. You have to take a look. There's this man who has been keeping an eye on us since the steamer ride and he's still there on the platform, as if he's been stationed there to watch us.'

Bimal leaped to the window. 'Where?'

'There he is!'

But the man had realized by then that he had been spotted. He hastily averted his face and vanished into the crowd.

Bimal said with a worried expression, 'Puzzling. Who is he?'

'Do you think he is one of Karali's spies?' I asked.

'Karali? But how will he know we're here today?'

'Perhaps he's worked out our plan. He guessed that we'd follow him sooner or later, probably within a few days. There is no other route to Assam. So he stationed a spy here.'

'Possible. Tell you what, let's get out and check if Karali's hiding in any of the compartments here,' saying this, Bimal stepped out of the compartment and on to the platform.

He returned just as the train was leaving.

'What did you see?' I asked.

'Nothing. I searched every single compartment with a fine-tooth comb. Karali's nowhere to be seen. Perhaps we're worrying too much.'

I was much assured by Bimal's words, but a niggling worry still remained at the back of my mind.

The train left the station.

'Kumar, take this chance to sleep as much as you can,' Bimal said. 'Once we reach Assam, we might not get a full night's sleep in a long while.' Then, with a happy 'Aaah', he stretched out on his bench and I went to sleep as well. Fortunately, we weren't sharing the compartment with anyone, so there was no fear of any disturbance during the night.

# 10

## Who Is This Thief?

We were standing in the middle of the Khasi Hills. In front of us, a stone Buddha idol. It was a pitch-black moonless night. There was darkness everywhere around us. High above, the stars twinkled, the contours of the hills around us could be seen dimly in their meagre light. The hills seemed like giants waiting in this half-light, like sentries to the doors of the ghost world, ready to pounce on us. Everything around us was so quiet that it gave me goose pimples. My heart leapt with foreboding at every moment!

Bimal said softly, 'This is the Buddha idol. This is where the treasure is.'

All at once, someone laughed—a taunting, gurgling laugh. The echo of that terrible, loud laugh seemed to leap over the tops of the hills and hop, skip and jump somewhere into the land of eternal darkness. I stood dumbfounded. Ramhari shrieked in terror and sat down, his hands covering his face. Bagha looked up at the midnight sky and howled pitifully.

Only Bimal was brave enough to call out, 'Who's there?'

Again that terrible, gurgling laugh. The entity behind the laughter could not be seen in the darkness, but it couldn't have been human. No human could laugh that repulsive laugh!

Bimal asked again, 'Who is this laughing?'

'It is *I*!' came the reply.

Ooh, what a deep voice it was!

'Who are you? Come and face us if you have any courage.'

'I *am* in front of you.'

'That's a lie! There is only the Buddha idol in front of me,' Bimal persisted.

'Ha! Ha! Ha! Ha! You think I am a Buddha idol? Look again, boy. I am the yaksha!'

The Buddha idol started moving, its eyes glowing red like hot coals. Bimal picked up his gun.

The idol laughed that gurgling laugh and said, 'Your bullets can do nothing to me.'

Bimal placed his finger on the trigger and said, 'We'll see about that.'

With a roar that made the very skies tremble, the idol shouted, 'Be warned! The stone on my body will shatter if you shoot. It will harm only you and yours.'

'Let it harm. I don't fear your harm.'

'I have been sitting here as guard for thousands and thousands of years. And you want to disturb my peace? You who were barely born yesterday? What do you want?'

'Treasure!'

'Ha! Ha! Ha! Ha! Treasure—you have high hopes! Do you know how many humans like you have died in their search for this treasure? Here, take a look at their bleached bones!'

In the glowing light of the idol's eyes, we saw an enormous pile of bones made of thousands of dead people on one side. Not in the least discouraged, Bimal said, 'Don't fob me off with all this. I want your treasure.'

'I shall not give it to you.'

'You must.'

'Never!'

'Then I shall blind you with my bullets.'

'You will be dead before you do that, boy!'

'You are just stone—immobile. How can you kill me? I am standing beyond your reach.'

'Ha! Ha! Ha! Look around you. My guards are everywhere! One order from me, and they'll squeeze you to death!'

'Where are these guards of yours?'

'Every hill here is my guard.'

'They are made of stone, too and cannot move, like you. Cut the drivel and hand over your treasure to me or watch me shoot you,' saying which, Bimal aimed with his gun.

'Die, then. Guards!' the idols glowering eyes went out. In the blink of an eye, some gigantic things leaped at us in the dark. A massive push hurled me to the ground and in unbearable pain I heard myself cry out 'Bimal! Bimal!'

I woke up. On opening my eyes, I saw that I had rolled off the bench on to the floor of the compartment. Bimal was leaning over my face, saying, 'There's nothing to fear, Kumar. The thief's escaped!'

My dream had still not left me, I said fearfully, 'The yaksha isn't there?'

Surprised, Bimal asked, 'What are you talking about, Kumar? What yaksha?'

I sat up, embarrassed and said, 'Bimal, I had a horrible dream. You'll marvel at the story when you hear it.'

Bimal said, 'What just happened inside this compartment was no dream. *You'll* marvel too when you hear it.'

Dumbfounded, I said, 'Inside this compartment? What happened here?'

'We were visited by a thief.'

'A thief? My word!'

'I suddenly woke up to find a man going through my bag. I jumped up immediately and landed a punch on his temple and he fell on you. And you let out a sort of strangled cry and fell off your bench on to the floor! The man was agile. He got up quickly, leaped out of the window and disappeared.'

'Leaped out of the window of a running train? He must be dead!'

'Probably not. The train was close to a station and running very slowly.'

'Did he take anything?'

'Yes! The skull,' said Bimal, and started laughing.

'Bimal, we've just lost the skull. And you're laughing?'

'Why shouldn't I? The thief's made off with the fake skull.'

'Fake skull! What's that?'

'Fine, I'll tell you. I had anticipated trouble of this sort on the way. That's why, before we left Calcutta, I procured a skull from a doctor in our neighborhood. I've engraved sums on this new skull as well, just like the old one. But these sums will set them off on a wild goose chase. I kept this fake skull in my bag. I was sure that if a thief tried to steal the skull, he'd be happy with this fake one. And so he was!'

'Bimal, thank heavens for your foresight! I had no idea you had thought this far ahead. Where is the real skull?'

'I got this bag specially made. My bag has a false bottom, rather like the hidden rooms that some houses have. The skull is in the hidden section.'

'Who do you think is this new enemy after us?'

'There is no new enemy, Kumar. This is Karali's work all right. He isn't fooled by my tricks. He must be hiding somewhere on this train.'

'There is that!'

'Kumar, are you scared again?'

'No, no, not scared, but I'm definitely worried.

What if this spy of Karali's had stabbed you in your sleep?'

'This happened because we had let our guard down thinking Karali wasn't travelling along with us. We'll be careful from now on. We'll keep Ramhari and Bagha close to us and we'll take turns sleeping.'

'Karali will attack us again as soon as he figures out he's got the fake skull.'

'And we'll be prepared for him! But there is no way he can figure out the forgery if he hasn't yet learnt how to decipher the code.'

The train was running breathlessly; moonlit fields and jungles flashed past our eyes like images in a bioscope. I couldn't trust myself to fall asleep again. I gazed outside instead and let my thoughts wander. With every minute, the train was taking us away…further away from our homeland. So many unknown, invisible dangers hanging over our heads! Who knows whether we'll ever come back home on this road again.

# 11

# Chhatak*

'Kumar, this is Sylhet,' announced Bimal as we reached there the next day.

'This is the famous birthplace of the Sylhet orange, isn't it?' I asked.

Bimal demurred and said, 'Well, oranges were not exactly born in Sylhet, but it is true that the river Surma carries boatloads of oranges from here to Calcutta. Why just oranges? Orange honey of Sylhet is known for its taste and its health benefits.'

I asked him, 'What else can be found in Sylhet?'

---

* Chhatak is a town in the north-east of Bangladesh, in Sylhet district, which is just south of Assam.

'Well, many crops, and cucumbers, pumpkins, pineapples, potatoes, cotton, sugarcane, bay leaves, chillies, spices and lime are exported from here. But the most interesting story is about the betel leaf and the betelnut of Sylhet.'

'Most interesting? Why?'

'Betel leaves aren't cultivated here like they are in Bengal; they grow in the wild. But the betel leaf vines and the betelnut trees are very friendly here. Walk into any wood or jungle and you will find betel leaves growing naturally in a grove of betelnut trees, the vine creeping up the tree. Other than that, sohphlang of Sylhet is famous!'

'Sohphlang! What's that?'

'A saffron-like root. A Khasi delicacy.'

We spent the entire day in Sylhet. We could see our destination, the Khasi hills, from here. Who knew what secrets it hid in its enormous heart? Once we stepped into those secrets, would we ever find our bearings again? This is nothing like hunting a house with an address and a number on a Calcutta street. Who knows where the yaksha's treasure is buried in this unending hill-forest-jungle journey? How on earth are we going to find it? Still, we were far more reassured than before since we saw no sign of Karali or his henchmen anywhere. I realized that the fake skull had satisfied Karali and so he no longer felt the need to guard us at all times. Long may it last! I hoped we'd get the job done by then and return to Calcutta.

We boarded the steamer at midnight and travelled up the Surma to reach Chhatak the next day.

Surma is the main river of Sylhet. Chhatak, too, lay on the banks of this river. We had heard of Chhatak's lime, but it was not actually from here. This lime was from the Khasi hills near Cherrapunji. From there, it would be loaded on to trains and boats and reach Chhatak and then from Chhatak, it would be exported all over. Cherrapunji did not just have lime. It had iron ore, its mines were rich with it. Two hundred and fifty odd years ago, large cannons were made from Cherrapunji iron. But no one in their right mind thinks of the iron in the Khasi hills now because of the bane of cheap foreign iron. The Khasi hills are also known for their coal, other than the lime and iron. But a weak transportation network means the coal is only used locally.

Chhatak isn't a bad place. It has a doctor, a police station, a post office, a market, a primary school—everything. There is also a dak-bungalow, which is where we put up for the night. Bimal told me that there was another small river here, which would take us up to Bholagunj. But because the river dries up at this time, the boat would go no further. So we would have to trek the mile and a half to Thariaghat, then climb the stone path up the Khasi hills. That night we were going to rest at the dak-bungalow and begin our journey the next day.

How beautiful the Khasi hills looked from Chhatak! Like an enormous blue cloud, they spanned my entire vision, spread out across most of the sky. There was no end to them. I had read about hills in books but never seen them with my own eyes and had no idea that hills could be so beautiful; I felt the Khasi hills beckoning me. I wanted to jump into their embrace in one sprint!

We chatted a bit in the evening and then turned in. It was nippy outside. I felt incredibly comfortable inside my quilt. Bimal got under his quilt as well and said, 'Sleep tight tonight, Kumar. Tomorrow at this time we will be in the hills. You won't be able to sleep so comfortably for a long time.'

'If we both sleep, who'll stand guard?' I asked.

'I've planned for that. Ramhari and Bagha are sleeping just outside the door, on the balcony outside. I have bolted all the doors and windows from the inside as well.'

My anxiety left me. Better safe than sorry, even though our enemies were nowhere in sight.

# 12

## Trouble Without Warning

I don't know how long I had been sleeping, but I woke up all of a sudden. Someone was sitting on my chest. I cried out Bimal's name in terror.

From the darkness, a hand grasped my throat and warned, 'Don't you dare! Make any loud noises, and I'll squeeze the life out of you.'

I went cold at this and said with difficulty, 'Let go of my throat. I'm suffocating.'

He removed his hand and said, 'Fine. But you're dead if you shout again.'

I couldn't see anything in that pitch-black darkness. Who was this sitting on my chest? I heard sounds of a scuffle in the other end of the room and then a groan as someone hit someone with something. Then, silence.

In that darkness, a hoarse voice asked, 'Shambhu, what's the matter?'

Another voice said, 'Babu, this lad has the strength of an ox. He would have pushed me off his chest. I had to use my stick to deal with him.'

'Have you finished him off?'

'No, he's just knocked out cold.'

'Good. Then let me switch on the light.' Saying which, he struck a match and lit the lamp. It was the man on the steamer and on the platform who had been shadowing us.

Seeing me stare at him, he laughed and said, 'So, partner? What makes you gawk? Or have you recognized me, by any chance?'

I didn't reply. There was still a man sitting on my chest. Bimal's body lay seemingly lifeless in another corner of the room. It was impossible to tell if he was dead or alive. I looked at the doors and windows, all shut as before. How did they come in then?

The man with the lamp walked up to me and said, 'Think you're very clever, don't you, boy? Finding the yaksha's treasure? What do you think will happen to you now?'

'Who-who are you?' I asked, now very scared.

'Why do you need these tedious introductions?'

'What do you want?'

'Pocketbook—pocketbook! We need your grandpa's pocketbook. We've got the skull already. Now be an angel and tell us where you've kept the pocketbook.'

I couldn't help but smile to myself even in the midst of such danger. So they thought the fake skull was the real thing! And they knew about the pocketbook, so they must be Karali's men.

Seeing my silence, the man threatened me and said, 'Cat got your tongue, lad? Tell us where the pocketbook is right away, or else…' He whipped out a dagger from his waistband. 'Do you see what I have here?' The blade glinted and flashed in the light of the lamp.

I hurriedly said, 'It's in that bag.'

'Hmm, that's the spirit, isn't it? Shambhu, open the bag and check.'

Shambhu was sitting next to Bimal's inert body. He walked over to the bag in the other corner of the room, tried to open the bag and said, 'It's locked.'

The man with the lamp turned to me once again and said, 'Where's the key to the bag?'

Before I could say anything, Bimal stood up like a whiplash and said, 'Here it is—I have it,' and raised his hand. He was holding a gun! I was stunned.

Bimal stepped in front and said, 'I will shoot the next man who moves a muscle.'

Suddenly, the man who held the lamp dropped it to the ground, plunging the room in darkness once again. With that, Bimal's gun spit fire with a loud bang. A man's voice yelled, 'Oh my god! I'm hit!' The man sitting on my chest let go. Immediately there was the sound of the door opening, Bagha's barking, Ramhari's voice. I couldn't understand what was going on. I just sat on the bed like a man hypnotized.

Bimal said, 'Kumar, light the lamp—quick!'

'But—but—'

'Don't worry. Light it. They're gone!'

I didn't have to light the lamp after all, as Ramhari hurriedly entered the room with a lantern.

There was no one other than us in the room.

Bimal went down on all fours on the floor and said, 'Blood stains. So the man escaped even after being shot. Perhaps the bullet just grazed his arm or something.'

Ramhari asked with an anxious expression, 'What's the matter, Babu?'

Bimal ignored him for the moment and continued, 'The door and windows were all shut from the inside, yet they got in. Oh, got it, they must have entered while we were in the dining room. The rascals hid under the bed all that time.'

I found this convincing as well. 'That makes sense. But Bimal, you were unconscious. How did you stand up all of a sudden?'

'I hadn't fainted at all. I was just pretending. Thank heavens the gun was on my bed!'

Just then, Bagha padded into the room, his tail wagging, and started licking my feet with great affection. I saw some stains around his mouth. They looked like blood! Was Bagha injured then? I hurriedly took my face close to his and realized, no, it was someone else's blood. Bagha must have taken a chunk off one of the goons!

I patted Bagha on the head and said, 'Well done, Bagha. Good boy!' Bagha seemed to melt with my praise and started rolling around near my feet in delight.

Bimal said, 'From now on, Bagha will sleep with us. A thing like this would never have happened had he been in the same room as us.'

'That is correct. But what plans for the future?

Karali will not let us go this easily. His spies will return in more numbers.'

Bimal said lightly, 'That they will.'

I persisted, 'And bear in mind that from tomorrow we will leave civilization behind and enter the hills. Who will rescue us there?'

Bimal struck the gun hard on the floor, raised one hand and said with fervour, 'Our own hands will rescue us! A person who cannot defend himself forfeits the chance to live!'

'But…'

'Forget about buts from today, Kumar—that is a word for cowards!' Saying this, Bimal pushed the window open with force and said, 'Look, Kumar!'

My eyes went to the window. Bathed in the moonlight of this still night, the Khasi hills seemed a vision from heaven. Such beauty, *such* beauty! Moonlight cascaded like waterfalls from peak after peak—light somewhere, shadow in others—like laughter and tears, side by side. Mesmerized, I stared at them. I had never seen anything as beautiful as this before.

Bimal asked, 'What are you looking at?'

I replied, 'A dream.'

Bimal said, 'No. It is reality! Do you want us to return from this heaven's door?'

I shook my head, 'No, Bimal. Never. We won't head back. I want to plunge into these hills, heart and soul! I don't care whether or not we get the treasure. I just want to go there once.'

Bimal shut the window and said, 'And so we shall, tomorrow. No more talking now. Let us turn in for the night.' Saying this, he put the gun beside him and stretched out on his bed. And started snoring forthwith. Looking at him sound asleep, who could say that we had just returned from death's door. I, too, banished all thoughts of danger from my mind when I saw his courage. Precisely when I dozed off, while thinking of the beauty of the Khasi hills, even I do not know.

# 13

# At the Khasi Hills

We crossed Cherrapunji and ventured further ahead on the road to Shillong. Cherrapunji to Shillong was about 32 miles. This distance was motorable, but we didn't take that option. Known routes came with the added risk of enemies.

Hill after hill—small, big, middling. Wherever I looked there were only mountains. Some of their peaks were really strange: they reached out like elephants' trunks as if they wished to pull down the blue sky and grind it under their enormous feet. These hills looked so harsh from afar, but on coming closer, I found them wrapped in silky blankets of green grass. Wild flowers bloomed all over them in groves, their beauty as dazzling as precious rubies, diamonds, sapphires. They seemed to be the hidden playgrounds of fairies. Somewhere little waterfalls tinkled down the terrain, leaping over rock after rock with their lullaby until they disappeared from view. Narrow pathways were flanked by deep gorges on either side, in which grew cinnamon trees by the hundreds, shivering in the cool breeze. Walking on these paths made one fear for every step—what if we skid and fell into the deep nothing below! Most striking of them all were the rows and rows of pine trees. I had never seen so many pine trees together before. They reigned all over the hillside. Unfettered by too many branches or creepers, they stood straight and proud, staring at the sky.

It was all very lonely, we only met some woodcutters on our journey. They were Khasi, the natives of these hills and resembled the gurkhas: flat noses, high cheekbones, arched eyes, small faces.

We were assured of one fact on this route after days spent trekking it: Karali's men did not know we had taken this path. I suppose they couldn't imagine we'd let go of the easier path and choose this way. Perhaps they were lying in wait for us in Shillong in vain. Served them right.

Bimal had hunted two pheasants earlier that day. As I walked on, I thought of how sweet their meat would taste.

The sun set, washing the western sky with vermillion. I said, 'Bimal, my legs are smarting after a long day's walk, my stomach's rumbling, too. Let's stop for today.'

'Why Kumar?' Bimal asked. 'Aren't you enjoying the scenic beauty anymore?'

'Oh, I am enjoying it all right. I can't get enough of it. But I have a hunch that I will enjoy warm pheasant meat a lot more right now!'

Chatting like this, we reached a small spring. Right next to it was a small cave.

Bimal said, 'Oh, that's a decent shelter. We can spend the night inside this cave. Ramhari, put the luggage here.'

We were all carrying some luggage or the other, which we kept inside the cave. It was quite a large one and would have held four or five more people easily.

Ramhari tidied up the dust and cobwebs a little, then asked, 'Khokababu, shall I now start cooking?'

'Yes. But let me show you something interesting first. You don't have to worry about lighting a fire here!' Saying which, he picked up an axe and walked into the brush. Ramhari and I started skinning the dead pheasants for cooking. Bagha sat close by, his tail wagging, his head cocked on one side, intently concentrating on the process. Clearly, his interest in the dinner menu was no less than ours!

Bimal returned a while later with a pile of dry twigs on his shoulder. 'Oh, just a pile of firewood. What's so interesting about that?' I remarked.

'Just watch,' said Bimal as he gathered some dry leaves towards himself, then lit a fire with his match. Then he held a twig over it and it burst into flames. Bimal held the twig up above his head like a flaming torch.

Fascinated, I asked, 'Amazing! What's this wood that lights up so easily?'

'Pinewood. Pine trees contain a sort of resin that makes them highly flammable. Which is why we also call them incense wood!'

That night, Ramhari cooked on pinewood. Bimal and I sat at the entrance of the cave and started chatting.

Dusk had ended by then, the half-moon was smiling at us from behind a nearby hill. In that half-light, the hills, the waterfall and the jungles seemed strangely unfamiliar.

Suddenly, Bimal asked, 'Kumar, do you believe in ghosts?'

'Why do you ask?'

'Many Khasis worship ghosts and spirits as gods. They sacrifice roosters and eggs to appease them. A land that has so many worshippers of ghosts must have a fair few, don't you think?'

'No, I don't believe in ghosts.'

'Why not?'

'Because I've never seen a ghost. Have you ever seen one?'

'No, but I know a ghost story.'

'What? A true story?'

'Don't know about that, but the person who told me the story insisted it was all true.'

'Who's he?'

'We had a neighbour, a tenant who rented one of the houses next door, now he's moved. His name was Ishaan.'

'Well, there's still some time to dinner. Why don't you tell me your story until then to pass the time? We'll decide whether I should believe it or not later.'

A freezing gust of wind came from nowhere. Both of us bundled ourselves tightly in our blankets. Bimal started his story in Ishaan's own words.

# 14

# Ishaan's Story

The Ganga is about four miles away from my village. So all deaths in the village would be cremated at the Ganga.

The time when Bhola's grandmother passed away, some five of us from the neighbourhood carried the corpse to the cremation ground. It was nearly midnight by the time we reached.

It is difficult to explain to you city dwellers what a cremation ground in a village is like. There are no gaslights here, no sound ever disturbs the silence. Many of them don't even have a hut for the bearers to wait in. They are open, lonely places, where the wind whistles past, jungles all around, you step on skulls and bones with practically every step. A midnight in these places can quell the sense of adventure in even the bravest hearts.

The cremation ground in our village, too, had one of these tumbledown, ramshackle huts. We placed the corpse with its bed in this. There is no readily available firewood in a village cremation ground, one has to get some from the nearby jungle.

Bhola said, 'Let me sit by the corpse. You all get the firewood.'

I asked him, 'Are you sure you won't be afraid on your own?'

Bhola was as devil-may-care as he was strong. He smiled dismissively and said, 'Afraid? What's afraid? Now go. Don't delay everything!'

The five of us entered the jungle and started chopping wood. It takes a lot of firewood to light a pyre. It took us nearly two and a half hours to chop enough firewood for the corpse. I realized that there would be no sleep for any of us tonight. The cremation would go on until dawn.

We were walking from the jungle together towards the cremation ground when someone said, 'Hey, look, look! The hut's on fire!'

And so it was. The hut was aflame. Taken by

surprise, we rushed towards the hut. As we neared it, we saw someone lying face down on the ground outside it. We hurriedly turned the man over to find it was none other than Bhola! He was foaming at the mouth, unconscious.

Bhola in a dead faint here, and the hut on fire there, nothing made sense. Mystified, we ran up to the entrance of the hut. Someone had heaped earth at the door until it was man height. Just a little higher and the entrance would have been completely sealed. Uncomprehending, we craned our necks to get a glimpse of the inside to see a pile of logs crackling with high flames in one corner, the stench of burning raw flesh and no sign of the corpse anywhere!

Nearly out of our minds with terror, worry and amazement, we returned to where we had left Bhola. After we had splashed his face several times with cold water, he slowly opened his eyes. What he said was this:

'You left to chop firewood and here I was, sitting alone with the corpse. After a while of sitting alone like this, I felt rather drowsy. I closed my eyes, allowing myself to nod off. Suddenly, there was a sound—plop! Startled, I woke up and looked all around, but there was no one. My mistake, I thought, leaned against the bedpost and tried to go back to sleep.

'The same plop! A little while later. This time I suspected it was a fox, tempted by the corpse. I didn't bother to open my eyes and some more time went by. This went on for a while: the complete silence followed by a periodic plop! Finally, annoyed beyond measure by this, I was forced to open my eyes. God help me! The door of the hut had nearly been sealed shut with earth, even the narrow escape route open would disappear in a bit. Who could have accomplished such a huge task in such a short time? My sleep left me in a trice, I quickly leaped over the mud wall and came outside.

'Everything was gleaming white in the moonlight. There was a dry stretch of the river between the hut and the Ganga. I looked around me and saw a man with bushy hair intently digging wet earth from the river bank with his bare hands. So it was him! But why do this? Was the man disturbed?

'As I thought this, the man walked to the hut with another pile of wet earth in his hands. He was enormous, with long beard and hair, practically naked, just a small scrap of cloth between his legs.

He had his head down, so he couldn't see me until I stood right in front of him.

'Then he raised his face and looked at me. Ooh! How terrible his eyes were—like two smouldering coals! I have never seen such firelit eyes in my whole life.

'I asked fearfully, "Who are you?"

'In reply, he shook his bushy head and let out such a horrific shriek that I felt the blood freeze in my veins. I ran away as fast as I could, but fell in a dead faint before I could go too far. Then I remember nothing.'

From Bhola's story we realized it was nothing but a Pishaach—a zombie-like flesh eater that enters corpses and brings them to life. When a corpse comes to life like this, it is called a Pishaach. It must have been the one who had burnt Bhola's grandmother and eaten half of her. He must have planned to eat Bhola too, just our timely arrival saved Bhola's skin!

We never did complete our cremation that time round.

# 15

# Two Burning Eyes

Bimal's story sent a chill up my spine. I couldn't bring myself to look outside the cave—who knows, perhaps there was someone hiding in the bushes, someone like that man in the story!

Bimal laughed at my expression and said, 'Hey, Kumar, are you afraid?'

'A bit, yes.'

'But you just said you don't believe in ghosts!'

'Hmm, yes. I didn't—but now I can't say for certain.'

'Don't be silly Kumar. There isn't a shred of truth in this. The whole thing's made up! A ghost story is nothing but a fairy tale, the insistence on ghosts being real is to make people believe the story.'

But I still wasn't convinced and didn't let Bimal stray far from me. In my fear, even Ramhari's fabulous pheasant meat tasted of nothing.

Bimal scattered pine logs around the cave and lit them, saying, 'No wild animal will be able to come over to our side over the fire. You two sleep for now. I'll keep guard this shift. Kumar, your turn will be after mine, then Ramhari's.'

Ramhari and I wrapped ourselves up and went to sleep.

At midnight, Bimal woke me up and said, 'Kumar, your turn!'

It was a wrench to leave the warm quilt on a cold night—especially in the middle of these hills and jungles. But there was no other option, so I had to. The fire outside the cave was dwindling, so I added a few more logs, cradled the gun and leaned against the wall of the cave.

The moon had set well before midnight. It was pitch dark outside! Wiping out the hills, jungles and shrubs was a limitless vista of darkness, and through that I could hear the restless murmurs of the waterfalls, the rustling of a hundred trees, the buzzing of a million cicadas.

Suddenly, I heard another kind of sound—just like the piercing wail of many newborn babies.

My heart jumped. How did so many newborn babies get here? I'd heard a horrible ghost story to begin with, then this pitch-black night in the belly of the jungle, then to top it all, this freakish wail! Many impossible thoughts arose in my mind.

That wail again. It sounded like the concert of a thousand ghostly babies, wailing in unison at the absence of their parents. I cowered in fear and shrank against the wall of the cave, when—what was that?

Just outside the cave, in the darkness, two smouldering eyes just like burning coal stared at me, unblinking. My heart stopped beating. These were just like the eyes of the Pishaach at the cremation ground—was this one, too?

Slowly, very slowly, the eyes advanced and then paused in the darkness, still staring at me. As if, in a sea of darkness, there floated two lumps of fire.

I could sit still no longer, I just picked up the gun with my trembling hands and somehow pressed the trigger. There was a loud bang and immediately the burning eyes went out!

Bimal, Ramhari and Bagha had all woken up at the sound of the gun going off. Bimal, flustered, asked, 'Kumar! Kumar! What happened?'

I said, 'Pishaach! It was a Pishaach!'

'What Pishaach?'

'Yes, it was! It stared at me with burning eyes and was coming closer, so I had to use the gun.'

Bimal took the gun away from my hands immediately. Then he grabbed the lantern, scaled the fire and went outside the cave to scan the surroundings. Returning, he said, 'There's nothing anywhere. You've lost your mind after hearing the ghost story, Kumar. You're imagining things!'

Just then, the ghost babies wailed again.

I blanched and said, 'There! You hear that?'

'What?'

'The ghost babies are wailing again. Ramhari, you've heard it too, haven't you?'

Bimal and Ramhari both burst out laughing. Furious, I said, 'What's so funny? Everything I've said so far seems funny to you two?'

Bimal spoke through gasps of laughter, 'Kumar, you've never stepped outside the limits of the city, so you know nothing of the world beyond it. You're just a full grown child! What you heard is not the wail of ghosts—that is the cry of young cranes!'

'Young cranes?'

'Yes! There must be a cranes' nest in some nearby tree. Young cranes sound a lot like human babies when they cry.'

I was terribly embarrassed. But what about those burning eyes? I hadn't imagined those! Bimal may dismiss them as much as he liked, but I could swear I had not imagined them and that I had seen them smoulder. With my own eyes.

# 16

# The Mystery of the Pishaach

We woke up the next morning to fresh trouble: Ramhari was down with a burning fever. So we had to stay on that day. There was no way Ramhari could hike with that kind of temperature. Constant moving had tired us as well, so I suppose it came as a welcome break.

Bimal hunted two wild fowl that day, which we cooked ourselves.

As dusk fell, my mind dwelled on last night's eerie incident. As soon as I mentioned it, Bimal laughed it off. But I couldn't shake the incident off my mind. I had seen it with my own eyes! God—it still made my hair stand on end!

That night, too, we lit a pinewood fire and closed the mouth of the cave. That night it would be Bimal and myself taking turns on the watch, for Ramhari was ill. Again, Bimal took over the first watch.

When my turn came, it was darkest night. The moon had set and from the depths of darkness, the waterfall's muted roar, the cry of the cranes, the murmur of the leaves and other unidentifiable sounds of the jungle reached my ears.

I threw some more logs into the dying fire in front of the cave; it was then that I heard a crackling sound. Someone or something was walking over the dry leaves outside. But try as I might, I couldn't see anything in the pitch darkness beyond the fire. The sound, too, stopped after a while. But my heart still beat a rapid tattoo in my chest.

Bagha was fast asleep, with his face buried in his stomach. I woke him. Bagha got up, and after a yawn and a stretch, came and sat next to me with his front paws outstretched. I put an arm around his neck and hugged him, and felt a bit reassured.

The same crackling sound again. I looked at Bagha, who had perked up his ears and was listening to the sound with his head cocked to one side. Then he rushed to the entrance of the cave in one leap and stood growling, because he couldn't go beyond the fire.

The growl woke Bimal. He sat up and asked, 'What's the matter? Why is Bagha growling like this?'

I said, 'There's a sound outside, someone is walking around.'

'What?!' said Bimal, taking the rifle from my hands.

The sound had stopped by then. But what was that? A pair of burning red eyes stared at us once again from the darkness!

Bagha started barking loudly, as I cried out, 'Look, Bimal, look!'

But Bimal had seen the eyes even before I had. He said nothing, just wordlessly aimed at the pair of eyes with his rifle.

The eyes were slowly creeping forward, when suddenly Bimal pressed the trigger.—There was a loud bang and an immense, terrifying roar. Then, silence. The eyes were no longer there.

Bimal turned to me and said, 'Did you see those eyes last night?'

'Yes. Now do you believe me?'

'Yes, I do. But they do not belong to any Pishaach. They are a tiger's.'

'Tiger?'

'Yes. Probably roared its last roar, but we can't say for certain. There's no need to go out of the cave tonight. If it isn't dead, an injured tiger is a very dangerous animal.'

The next morning, we woke up and saw that Bimal was spot on. At a little distance from the cave, a dead tiger was sprawled out on the hills. We measured and found it was a full five feet tall. Bimal's aim was marvellous, the bullet had struck the tiger right between the eyes!

# 17

# In the Jaws of Death

In about three days, Ramhari's fever went down, and we resumed our journey. Once again, we snaked the edge of the hills in search of our unknown adventure.

Bimal said, 'I'll walk on ahead. We need to find our ration for the day. Let me see if I can find any wild fowl.' And he marched on ahead, gun slung over his shoulder. After a while, we lost sight of him in the many bends of the snaking path, but we could still hear his booming voice singing:

'Move on, move on, brother!
To languish in the rear, to die in vain out of fear –
What matters if we live or die, brother!'

After a while, the singing faded into the distance.

Ramhari was still quite drained from his fever and couldn't walk fast, so I had to stay back with him.

The morning light stole my heart that day. It felt like someone had spread liquid gold over the hills like a beaming, sweet smile. Birdsong rang through the hills, the wind blew through the trees making waves of green, clumps of wild flowers bloomed carelessly in odd corners in great profusion, nodding their heads affectionately as if to say, 'make garlands out of us, caress us, remember us—never forget us.'

The young blooms seemed to me like the offspring of the forest gods. I picked so many, but how much can one carry? There were more flowers than an emperor's garden could hold.

There are many species of flowers just like these in all countries, not just ours. But we do not care to find out about the immense variety of flora that our own land is host to. Like fools, we sit in our little corners and these species are looted by westerners. Then they are sold in fashionable flower markets and hothouses at exorbitant prices and are bought mainly by white people. This alone tells me that not only do we lack business acumen, but the most shameful thing of all, we have not learned to value and respect the wealth of our own nation.

I was mulling over all this and walking along, when Ramhari suddenly cried out, 'Chhoto Babu, look, look!'

I turned around and asked, 'What?'

Ramhari pointed at the ground with his forefinger.

A rifle lay abandoned on the track. One look and I recognized it as Bimal's.

I stood on the path and wondered why Bimal would leave his rifle in the middle of the path and where he could go. It was not at all like him. It all looked very fishy, something had definitely gone wrong. Then I looked up to see Bagha sniffing a spot near the path and whining.

I stepped up to the spot and realized there was a small pool of blood there.

Ramhari, close to tears, said, 'Khokababu must be in some kind of danger.'

I said, 'Looks like it, Ramhari. But exactly what kind of danger?'

Ramhari replied, 'How can I guess, Chhoto Babu? These hills hold tigers and bears, so many predators.'

'Tigers and bears are predators, but they don't

steal bags, Ramhari. It wasn't a tiger; otherwise his bag would have been here along with his rifle.'

'Then where did Khokababu disappear?' Ramhari said, preparing to call out.

I quickly stopped him. 'Hush, don't shout out his name. I believe he has fallen into the enemy's hands, and that they are nearby. We will fall into the same danger if we shout now.'

'What should we do then?'

'You stay hidden in the bushes. Leash Bagha and don't let him bark. I shall walk on ahead and look around.'

Ramhari attached the leash to Bagha's collar and hid behind one of the clumps of bushes next to the trail.

At first, I couldn't tell which way to turn. But after a little distance I noticed that there were bloodstains on the trail, and a little further on, another bloodstain. Right after the third bloodstain on the tracks, the trail abruptly narrowed next to a bush, and on that trail was a narrow straight mark on the ground, as if someone had dragged a heavy load over it.

I followed the narrow trail and found that the bloodstains showed up every now and then. I knew instinctively that I would find Bimal at the end of those bloodstains. But would I find him alive? Was that blood his? Who were the people who had dragged him away? Were they robbers? My questions found no answers.

I stopped in my tracks suddenly. I heard voices speaking very close by.

I checked the rifle in my hands once. There were still two bullets in it. Then I bent low next to the bushes and slowly crept closer.

I didn't have to go far; where the narrow trail ended, there, a small clearing and right after that, a gorge!

I will never forget what I saw that day. Six men stood around the clearing. I recognized one of them instantly—Karali. On the far side, under a tree leaning towards the open gorge, lay Bimal. His head and face were bleeding; his arms and waist tied with ropes. Pinning Bimal down was one of Karali's henchmen.

I heard Karali say in a loud voice, 'Bimal, there's still time to answer my question. The pocketbook is not inside your bag; tell me where it is.'

But Bimal did not answer.

Bimal remained silent.

Karali said, 'Shambhu.'

The man pinning Bimal down turned and said, 'Yes, sir.'

I recognized the man. I had seen him at the dak-bungalow at Chhatak.

'Look here, Shambhu, if Bimal does not answer me in the next sixty seconds, throw him into the gorge,' Karali said.

A few seconds passed. My heart started beating a rapid tattoo; I was at my wits' end and couldn't understand what to do.

Karali said, 'Bimal, this is my last warning. You realize what will happen to you if you don't obey? Your body will be ground to dust without a trace after falling a thousand feet.'

Bimal stayed mum.

I couldn't bear it any longer. I decided I would step up and tell Karali what he needed to know. There's no need for the yaksha's treasure, life is a far greater treasure than money. I made up my mind and stood up from my hiding place.

Karali said, 'Bimal, you are still silent?'

After all this while, Bimal spoke. 'Will you let me go as soon as you find the pocketbook?'

Karali said, 'Certainly.'

'If you search in the inside pocket of one of my jackets, you will find the pocketbook.'

The jacket was lying at Karali's feet, a little search and it was found.

Karali's face broke into a monstrous triumphant smile.

But even in the middle of all this danger, I smiled at his false victory. For I knew that Bimal had already erased the path to the treasure. He had not lost his head for a moment, bless him!

Bimal said, 'Now that you have got your wish, let me go.'

Karali said in a harsh croak, 'Yes, that is what you would say. Leave no trace of your enemies, I say. Shambhu, throw the boy over the ledge.'

Bimal yelled, 'Karali! Shaitan! You...'

But before he could finish his sentence, Shambhu dragged him to the edge of the gorge and pushed him over in one heave and before I could so much as blink, Bimal's body dropped down and disappeared without a trace.

A veil of darkness appeared before my eyes and as I fell to the ground with my head spinning, I heard Karali's terrible roar of laughter! Immediately after, I lost all consciousness.

# 18

## A Miraculous Thing

I have no idea how long I had fainted. When I regained consciousness, I opened my eyes to find Ramhari leaning over me, intently looking at my face. Seeing me open my eyes, he heaved a big sigh of relief and said, 'Chhotobabu, what happened? What made you faint?'

I couldn't recall what at first. I sat up slowly—disoriented and dumbstruck.

Ramhari said, 'I was very worried when you didn't return. I tied up Bagha at the spot and came to find you—'

I remembered at last. I interrupted Ramhari and rambled, 'Ramhari, Ramhari—I will kill them!'

Surprised, Ramhari asked, 'Who will you kill, Chhotobabu? What are you going on about?'

Picking up my gun from the ground, I said, 'The men who threw Bimal into the gorge.'

'Khokababu has been thrown into a gorge? What?' said Ramhari and started to wail loudly.

'This is no time for tears, Ramhari!' I said. 'First, we want revenge. Now get up, take Bimal's gun and come with me.' Saying this, I came out of the bushes. I had decided I'd shoot the first person I lay my eyes on.

But there was no one anywhere! The space beside the gorge was empty, not a soul was to be seen.

From behind me, Ramhari asked again, 'Who do you want to shoot, Chhotobabu?'

I said between gritted teeth, 'Karali! But where did he disappear with his troops in such a short time?'

'Karali?' a stunned Ramhari could say no more.

'Yes Ramhari, Karali. Bimal has been thrown into the gorge on his orders.'

Weeping inconsolably, Ramhari asked, 'Where did they throw Khokababu from?'

Tears choked my voice as well. Somehow I controlled them and said in a lacklustre voice, 'Ramhari, there is no point in looking for Bimal.

They have thrown him from that precipice with his hands and feet bound. That height would grind iron to dust, a human body stands no chance! We will never set eyes on Bimal again.'

Ramhari struck his forehead with his palm and said, 'How will I ever show my face to Ma Thakurun without Khokababu? No, I will not live either. I, too, shall jump into the gorge.' Saying this, he ran to the precipice. I restrained him with great trouble. Thereafter he lay on the ground and sobbed his heart out.

I stood at the edge of the cliff from where they had thrown Bimal over. Then I leaned over to see if I could see Bimal's body anywhere.

My head spun as soon as I looked down. I had never seen such a deep gorge, ever! It went down steep, vertical from the edge of the hill, I couldn't tell how far below, until it disappeared into a misty haze at the bottom.

Suddenly, something strange caught my eye. Some thirty feet below the spot where I stood, a thick shrub grew outwards from the cliff face and on that bush—what was that? It looked like a human form!

I yelled with all my might, 'Bimal! Bimal!'

A voice replied from below, 'Kumar, I'm still alive, my friend.'

I nearly fainted a second time—this time out of sheer joy. Ramhari started dancing beside me, delighted. However, I controlled myself with effort and said, 'Ramhari, our dancing like this will not do, we have to get Bimal back up here!'

Ramhari immediately stopped dancing, scratched his head and with worried, rounded eyes said, 'We must, Chhotobabu. But how do we go down there? There is no path!'

I peeped and saw that it was impossible to reach Bimal. No man could climb down that sheer cliff face—we are not lizards! But there Bimal was, with a thousand feet of gorge below him, resting on an insignificant little shrub.

Bimal's voice shouted from below, breaking my reverie. 'Kumar, you must lift me right away. I'm sliding down steadily!'

I quickly peered over the edge and asked, 'But how will we reach you, Bimal?'

Bimal said, 'There is a rope in my bag, lower it to me.'

'But your hands and feet are tied. How will you hold on to the rope?'

'Kumar, don't waste time like this. Just lower the rope right away!'

Bimal's bag was lying where it was. Thank goodness Karali's men hadn't taken it with them. Ramhari immediately got a coil of thick rope from it.

A strong breeze was blowing, and with every gust, the shrub swung from side to side and every time, Bimal's body inched closer to the fall. What a terrible situation to be in! My heart started pounding in fear.

Bimal said, 'Bring the rope down to my mouth. Once I get a good grip on it with my teeth, you two pull me up.'

I had once seen a white man lift a hundred kilos in a circus with his teeth. I knew Bimal was very strong, but were his teeth strong enough to hoist him up?

A sudden strong gust of wind pushed Bimal's body even lower towards the fall. He somehow hung in there by contorting his body. It was now a matter of seconds. I could guess the state of his mind with one look at his ashen face. One more gust and we would not be able to save Bimal.

I lowered the rope as fast as I could. Bimal bit on it with all his strength. Ramhari and I started pulling the rope together. Soon Bimal's body was at the edge of the cliff; his face had turned brick red by then. His life now depended on the strength of his teeth alone.

Ramhari said, 'Chhotobabu, can you hold on to the rope by yourself for a little while? I can then pull Khokababu up.'

I said, 'Yes.'

Ramhari ran to Bimal and pulled him up. Ramhari let go only when Bimal was far clear of the precipice and safe. Then he hugged Bimal right there and started weeping with joy and relief. I went across and opened his bonds.

'Bimal, how did you get into their hands?' I asked.

Bimal said, 'I was singing along, lost in my own world, when I got ambushed. They were hiding at the side of the path in the bushes, I think. They hit me on the head from behind, and I fainted.'

'I saw the rest. I never thought we would ever get you back.'

Bimal smiled and said, 'Yes. By now, I could actually have been touring the underworld. But thank goodness the shrub was right under my feet! Divine protection, eh?'

I pleaded with him, 'Bimal, let's not go after the

yaksha's treasure any more. Why don't we go back home with our lives intact?'

Bimal said, 'I'm not a coward like you. You go back if you want to. I will not budge until I see this affair to its rightful end.'

# 19

# Trouble Among the Trees

Our trekking had begun again. This time round, we walked as fast as we possibly could. Now that the enemy was on our tail, the faster we arrived at our destination, the safer it was for us.

It wasn't possible to keep track of the number of jungles, woods, peaks and valleys that we crossed on our way. At times I felt as if we were all born to trek through life, we walk and walk through it until the day we die. In peak afternoons, when the hills heat up like a frying pan, we would halt, cook something, have lunch and rest for a while. We were forced to take a break on those nights when there was no moonlight. Otherwise, every day we saw the first blush of dawn, then the sun emerging like an enormous disc of vermilion, the whole world waking to the call of the forest birds, the sun's farewell at the hint of dusk with a mass of clouds at the rainbow-hued horizon, then the emergence of the moon like a sky lantern released by the fairies. The same moon would fade away in front of our eyes on so many nights when it sensed the dawn—just like an illusion.

But why were there no signs of Karali? We should have met him by now because he must have understood in all this time that the pocketbook had no information! Had he given up and finally stopped following us, or was he going to cross our path one day?

We trekked on like this, until one day, we stood in front of the entrance to the Roopnath cave. So this was it! I had heard that one go could go through this cave and reach all the way to China. Legend has it that once a Chinese emperor had come through this route to attack India. Of course, this is hardly a historical fact. Anyway, it doesn't really matter if the Roopnath cave was big or small, we needn't worry about that at all. But we heaved a collective sigh of relief once we reached here because this had been our destination for all these days. At least we knew now that we would see this adventure through to the end, because the place where the yaksha's treasure was hidden was very close from here, a two- to three-day journey, at most.

Bimal sat smiling under a tree, humming. I went across to him and said, 'Bimal, it is rather premature to celebrate.'

Bimal frowned and said, 'Why?'

'Suppose we go all the way to the Buddhist monastery and find that the treasure isn't there, then?'

'Why won't it be there?'

'How do we know that the hermit who gave Thakurda the skull wasn't fibbing in the first place?'

'No, I firmly believe the hermit was telling the truth. He had nothing to gain from an unnecessary lie.'

I didn't argue any more.

Bimal said, 'Don't worry your head with all these negative thoughts. For now, just rest here. Tomorrow we'll start walking towards the Buddhist monastery.'

The sun had set, but it was yet to get dark. The western sky still looked like someone had dappled paint playfully all over it. The breeze felt sweet on my skin. Bimal was humming to himself and I was listening in silence—his singing called for that. Some time passed like this.

My wandering glance fell on the jungle in front. At once, the hair on my skin rose. I clearly saw Karali's horrible face peeping at us from behind a tree. His tiny, close-set eyes were filled with hatred, like a snake's. As soon as it met my eyes, the face disappeared like lightning among the trees.

I squeezed Bimal's arm urgently; startled, he stopped singing.

I whispered, 'Karali.'

Bimal rose to his feet in one leap and asked, 'Where?'

I pointed to the tree in the jungle and said, 'There.'

Bimal immediately headed off in that direction, but I stopped him and said, 'No, don't go. Perhaps his men are hidden there as well. You might be inviting trouble.'

Bimal said, 'You're right. But I can barely contain myself, Kumar! I feel like rushing up to him and squeezing his neck with my bare hands.'

I said, 'No, no. Let's move from here instead. Let Karali continue to think we haven't spotted him. It'll buy us some time to think about what we should do next.'

Casting a wary eye on our surroundings, we moved on. With Karali and his henchmen this close to us, we were aware that fresh danger would arrive shortly. The sense of joy that we had felt on arriving so close to the treasure had evaporated like camphor with the sight of Karali's face. What a pain—is there no escape from the maws of this Rahu?*

* Rahu is one half of the mythical pair of Rahu-Ketu, a truncated demon who swallows the sun and the moon to cause eclipses. Rahu as a word is also used to denote a persistent obstacle or an obsessive enemy.

# 20

# Obstacle

This was one inaccessible path! Sometimes it went up as steep as a cliff, sometimes it dipped low towards hell, it twined itself around peaks and went through pitch-black caves. No one must be using it, because thorny bushes grew all over it in such profusion that it was impossible to pass without cutting our way through with axes. Had Thakurda's pocketbook not mentioned this path in such detail, we would never have found our way through it. It's true that we no longer had the pocketbook with us, but we had both copied down the code and kept a copy with each one of us.

We couldn't progress at a fast pace because the

path was in such poor condition. Trekking twenty miles in twenty-four hours was not difficult for either of us, but the same stretch on this route took us exactly five days.

Since yesterday it seemed as if there were no other humans in this world but us. Everything was so silent around us that we were startling ourselves with the sound of our own footsteps. Each time Bagha barked, the echo from the hills would be so frightening that it seemed the peaks had suddenly woken up at the sound of our footsteps and were now flying away helter-skelter with great commotion, for they had never ever seen humans walk this path before.

On the fifth day, just before sunset, a scene of unprecedented beauty met our eyes. In the distance we saw rows of temple-like structures, jet black, as if an invisible hand had brushed them with black ink and set them against a flame-coloured sky. The temples had been built on a high mountain peak. The sight of the temples crowning the peak of this quiet land with such gravitas was so awe-inspiring that we were stunned into silence for a while.

Bimal spoke first. He shouted out in glee, 'The Buddhist monastery!'

I shouted too, 'The yaksha's treasure!'

Ramhari said, 'Our hard work of all these days has finally paid off.'

Bagha didn't understand a word of what we said of course, but what he did glean was that we were all very happy. Wagging his tail and barking loudly, he joined in the celebrations as well.

We overcame our first rush of joy and walked ahead hurriedly. The monastery was still a mile or so away in the distance. We resolved to rest only when we reached the place.

Dusk gathered around us and gradually darkened into night. Bimal was leading the way. Suddenly he stopped and said, 'Disaster.'

I said, 'What's the matter, Bimal?'

Bimal said, 'Ooh, we just got saved from certain death.'

'Why? What happened?'

'Halt! Do not advance a single step! There's been a landslide. There's no path ahead.'

Thunderstruck, I considered this: no path ahead! What was Bimal saying? Very carefully, I went ahead a step or two and gave up all hope. Slap bang in the middle of the path the hill had disappeared in a massive landslide, leaving behind a fifty- to sixty-feet-deep gap that was about eighteen-feet wide!

Everything around us was so steep that there was no way we could climb into the gap and climb back up again. What cruel irony was this? After so many days, having surmounted so many difficulties and reached the location of the yaksha's treasure, would we have to return empty handed?

My whole body felt listless all of a sudden. I slumped down on the ground.

I raised my face after a while and found Bimal staring at a pine tree next to the spot where the path had disappeared.

I said, 'What is left to see there, Bimal? Come, sit here, let's rest here tonight and start heading back tomorrow.'

Bimal said in an angry voice, 'If we mean to give up so easily, why did we even bother to be born as human beings?'

'What option is there but to give up? We can't very well leap across it and we don't have wings for flying, either.'

'I'm not asking you to leap or fly. We will walk across it.'

Surprised, I said, 'Walk across? How?'

'I'll tell you. This gap isn't more than seventeen or eighteen feet, right?'

'Right.'

'Well, how tall do you reckon the pine tree beside the gap is?'

'Far more than seventeen or eighteen feet.'

'Great, then what do we have to worry about? We'll chop the tree at the base in such a way that it falls across the gap when it's felled. You realize what happens then, don't you?'

Delighted, I jumped up and exclaimed, 'Oh—got it! The tree will fall across the gap and make a small bridge across it. And we can easily go across. Bimal, you are a veritable god of intelligence—you are Brihaspati. Compared to you, I'm an idiot.'

Bimal said, 'Everyone is intelligent, but the trouble starts when people can't keep their heads cool in a crisis. Anyway, we rest here tonight. Tomorrow we must fell the tree.'

# 21

# Obstacle upon Obstacle

It was the darkest night. We were sheltering under a bit of the mountain that jutted out. There were hills on either side of us and fire, too, that we'd lit for protection. Bimal and Ramhari were fast asleep, wrapped up in their blankets. I was wrapped up as well, but I wasn't sleeping. It was my turn to keep watch.

The moonlight was feeble that night. Light and shadow seemed to be playing hide and seek all around me.

Suddenly a small animal, probably a fox, ran across the path to the monastery, looking behind again and again. It seemed the animal was running from something or someone. It made me suspicious. I covered myself from head to foot in the blanket, but left a small gap near my eyes to keep watch. I kept my gun at the ready under the blanket as well.

One, two, three minutes went by. Then I saw a man emerge from behind the hill on to the path… then another…then another…then two together. All told, five men. They were tiptoeing towards us like thieves in the dead of night. Even though I couldn't recognize them in the darkness, I could guess who they were.

The man in front had come really close to us. The flame of the fire in front of us lit up his face and I immediately recognized Karali! My heart danced with a cruel joy. Here he was! We had gone through countless troubles because of him. We had nearly lost our lives because of him and he was ready to finish us off yet again. He had slipped through our fingers many a time, but tonight I wouldn't let him go.

Keeping the gun close, I lay as stiff as a corpse. Let Karali come closer. I shall end his dreams of finding the treasure once and for all!

Gradually, Karali tiptoed to within thirty feet of where we were, his four henchmen following close behind.

In the light of the fire, I saw Karali's face assume a demonic expression. His right hand held a large, shiny dagger—to stab us in the chests with, no doubt. His followers too were armed with a spear, dagger and a sword each. We were truly fortunate that none of Karali's men could get hold of a gun. Had they been able to do so, we would not have remained alive till now.

Now Karali was about to cross our fire barricade. I realized it was time. I stood up like lightning then pulled the trigger in the blink of an eye. Bang! Karali raised his hands above his head and fell to the ground with a terrible cry. His men were stunned, I fired another shot in their direction and they ran for their lives.

But the bullet had perhaps only grazed Karali, for he stood up in a moment and then ran as fast as he could, disappearing into the darkness. My double-barrelled gun had no more bullets left, so I couldn't stop him. A few seconds after this, a bloodcurdling shriek reverberated through the silent night sky. I had never heard such a cry before ever in my life. Then, silence again. What just happened?

All this happened in seconds. By then, Bagha, Bimal and Ramhari had also woken up due to the commotion. I explained everything to Bimal as fast as I could, then said, 'But I don't understand where that shriek came from. It sounded like some three people cried out together.'

Bimal said gravely, 'Oh how terrible! Blinded by the darkness, they must have fallen into the gap in the broken path! They must all be dead by now.'

I said, 'But Karali did not go in that direction. He is still alive.'

Ramhari said, 'I feel bad for the scoundrels. Such a terrible fate in the end.'

Bimal said, 'They deserved it, no doubt. There is no point in mourning their loss. If Karali doesn't learn from this then he, too, will face a similar fate.'

'At least for a few days we will be rid of Karali. He isn't dead, of course, but there is no doubt he is seriously injured,' I added.

Bimal said, 'If we can work unhindered for three more days, the yaksha's treasure will be in our hands. I promise you that.'

I smiled. 'Hear! Hear!'

# 22

# Supernatural

We hacked away at the base of the pine tree the next morning, taking care to cut in such a way that the tree would land right across the gap when it was finally felled.

It started swaying at around noon. We started to work very carefully then, all our hopes now resting on this tree. One miscalculation and we would have to return empty-handed. There was not much time left for the tree to fall. Its base was beginning to crack.

Bimal said, 'A few more chops, and we're done.'

I aimed and hacked at the base a few more times.

Bimal said, 'Careful. Move away, it's falling.' Ramhari and I leapt to one side.

Crack—crack—craaaaack! The tree hurtled downwards towards the gap.

Bimal said, 'Done. Look, Kumar. Our bridge's ready.'

The tree had fallen neatly across the gap in the middle, its base on this side and the branches at the other. Just as we had wanted.

We finished lunch, rested for a bit and then set out for the Buddhist monastery. The hilly track had heated up unbearably in the afternoon sun, but we ignored all that, resolving instead to rest only once we reached the monastery.

It was nearly dusk now. The monastery wasn't far either. The cloud-kissed broken peak of its temple was getting clearer. We could also see some smaller ruins around it from where we were.

On walking closer, we found many carved stone caves on either side of us. Buddhist monks would have lived here once; now there was no sign of life.

The path between the caves had sharply swerved to one side. We stood at that bend: the main gate of the monastery was right in front.

We cheered loudly in unison. Bagha, who didn't

understand our cause for celebration, also barked loudly. The ruined temple and its surroundings came alive after ages with our noise.

Bimal raised both hands in the air and shouted, 'The yaksha's treasure! It's ours now!'

I said, 'Come on. Let's first find the spot.'

The main gate opened into the courtyard of the temple. It was an enormous courtyard, with rooms set out in a neat square formation around it, but not much of the earlier grace and beauty remained. Wild weeds had overrun the place, making it difficult to step in. Broken idols and loose stones lay here and there. There were animal skeletons in places, too. Perhaps wild animals now resided in the cells of the monks, bringing in their prey here to eat in peace.

I said, 'Bimal, take the skull out now. We have to figure out the rest of the path from the message.'

Bimal said, 'Not to worry. I remember the message by heart,' then recited, 'Behind the broken shrine, the pine tree. From the trunk base, ten yards east. Stop. Go right eight yards. Buddha in the east. To the left six yards ahead, three rocks. Dig under for seven cubits and find your path.'

I said, 'So first we need to search for the broken shrine.'

'Why should we search? The broken shrine here must refer to the main temple. That's broken, too. Let's just try it out, anyway.'

We walked to the rear of the main temple.

Ramhari said, 'Wonderful! You were right, there it is, the pine tree behind the broken shrine.'

True. There was a large clearing behind the main temple, and in it grew a solitary pine tree. There was no possibility of confusing it with any other.

All around us were scattered a multitude of Buddha idols—some seated, some standing, small and big ones. There were also rocks all around, both broken and unbroken.

Bimal said, 'Our treasure lies with one of these many idols. Okay, so I walk ten yards to the east from the pine tree and I stop. Now, eight yards to the right…hmm… Here it is, the idol of Buddha. To the left now for six yards, Kumar—look! Three rocks arranged in a line, just as it is described in the message. So the message on the skull wasn't a lie!'

My heart swelled with emotion and relief. Unable to bear it any longer, I slumped down on the stones.

'Up, up!' Bimal said. 'Now we have to check if there is actually anything under the rocks.'

The three of us immediately put our shoulders to

the task and removed the stones, proceeding then to dig under. After digging for about seven cubits, something hard struck our axe again and again. On removing some more earth, we found another large stone.

A bit of effort from the three of us and the stone was easily removed—and immediately we saw a gaping hole, with steps going down one side.

Our feelings at that moment were indescribable. We sat and stared at each other in silent, bewildered joy.

But something jolted us awake from this happy state of affairs. Smoke was billowing out of the hole in the ground in great gushes.

'Bimal, look, look!'

Bimal fixed his eyes on the hole in amazement and said, 'What on earth is this? How is it possible for smoke to billow out of a hole that has been sealed for so long?'

There was not much time left for dusk. Darkness had started collecting in clumps near the bushes and the crevices of the hills. Everything was so silent that we couldn't even hear a bird cry. The smoke was still billowing out of the hole, curling in large spirals as it moved up towards the sky.

Bimal softly said, 'Night is upon us. Let's not bother right now. We'll check it out tomorrow morning. Come, let us seal the mouth of the hole again.'

# 23

# The Death Laugh

A sense of foreboding came over me. How did smoke come from a pit that had been sealed off with so many stones? There could be no smoke without fire, but could there be fire inside that pit either? No amount of thinking gave me any sensible answer.

That night we took shelter inside one of the rooms. After dinner, just before we went to bed, I asked Bimal, 'Hey, do you believe yakshas exist?'

'I've heard they're some sort of spirit creatures who protect hidden treasure. But I have never seen one with my own eyes, so I don't believe they exist,' Bimal replied.

'You haven't seen god with your own eyes either, but if you can believe in the divine, why can't you believe in yakshas in the same way?'

'Why this sudden obsession with yakshas, Kumar?' Bimal asked.

'Because I believe the pit with the treasure in it also contains some sort of a ghost or spirit in there, otherwise—'

'Hang *otherwise*. I'm going into that pit tomorrow morning, ghost or no ghost.'

Bimal said these last words in a firm voice and wrapped himself up in his blanket, ending the discussion.

But the flutter of fear in my heart didn't leave me. I sat as close to Ramhari as I possibly could and asked, 'So Ramhari, do you believe in yakshas?'

'I do, Chhotobabu.'

'Don't you feel, Ramhari, that there's a yaksha inside that pit?'

'Whether it's a yaksha or a rakshas, a ghost or a spirit, I will go wherever Khokababu goes,' said Ramhari, then he, too, stretched out on the ground to sleep.

Like servant, like master! Both as stubborn as mules. Hapless, I sat guard at the entrance of the cave.

We returned to the pit at the crack of dawn. We removed the rocks from the entrance once again. Then we waited for a while, but no smoke emerged.

Relieved, Bimal said, 'Perhaps there was steam build-up because it had stayed shut for so long and we just mistook it for smoke.'

I agreed. Much calmer, I asked, 'What should we do now?'

Bimal said, 'We'll go into the pit, then hunt for the treasure. Kumar, Ramhari, each of you pick up a torch, because it will be as dark as night inside the tunnel.' Saying this, he entered the pit with Bagha. Ramhari and I followed.

Ooh, it really was as dark as night inside! Once we had moved in a few steps, we forgot that it was broad daylight outside. Thank goodness for the electric torches, or we wouldn't have been able to advance a single step.

As we went further inside, we had to double up, because the ceiling of the tunnel was so low that there was no way to stand up straight.

Suddenly, there was some sort of a sound behind us. We stopped immediately.

Turning back, we saw that the light at the end of the tunnel behind us could not be seen any more.

That same sound again, then once again and again.

I ran to the entrance of the tunnel. My heart leapt to my mouth when I saw what had happened.

The entrance had been sealed shut.

Bimal came running too and watched the sealed entrance in silent horror.

For a while we were all silent; Ramhari was the first to speak. 'Who did this?'

Bimal started to push against the door with all his might. But even his strength had met its match today. The door did not budge an inch.

I lost all hope and said, 'Bimal, let it go, there is no hope of our ever escaping this place. Be prepared to be buried alive.'

No sooner than I'd spoken, that a voice like a clanging metal canister giggled out loud. My heart sank at the sound of that horrible, metallic laughter.

The sound of the laughter was coming from within the tunnel. All three of us flashed our torches at it, but we could see nothing.

'Who laughed, Kumar?' Bimal asked.

Shaking like a leaf, I croaked, 'The yaksha! It's him!'

And immediately, that clanging, metallic giggle again.

No human can laugh like that. Even Bagha cocked his ears and listened intently while he stared into the depths of the tunnel.

I covered my ears with my hands and sat down on the floor of the tunnel. Anything but the sound of that laugh.

# 24

## The Treasury

I had never heard such a spine-chilling laugh in all my life—it would have made a corpse tremble. The entire tunnel seemed to reverberate with its sound.

It seemed to me that the yaksha had started giggling in glee on finding humans in its pit after many years, for food had walked right into its hands after so many years of starvation.

The mouth of the tunnel above us was shut—and this horror was going on inside. Undoubtedly, we would never see the sun or the moon again in this lifetime.

The sound of laughter gradually receded into the

distance. Only its echo bounced around the walls again and again.

I doubt if any other Bengali boy my age had faced danger of this magnitude before. It was a wonder I hadn't gone mad with terror. The three of us sat stunned on the ground and looked at each other with blank expressions. No one could speak.

For the first time ever, I saw Bimal look worried. I couldn't tell if he was afraid, but he did look considerably demotivated. Surely, only a superhuman being could remain motivated in the face of all this?

Ramhari spoke first. He pulled me up by the hand and said, 'Babu, it won't do to sit around like this. Surely we ought to do something?'

I said, 'What on earth can we do? Let's just sit here and breathe helplessly for as long as we still have our lives.'

Bimal said, 'But who closed the mouth of the cave?'

I said, 'The yaksha.'

Bimal made a face at this. 'To hell with your yaksha! I don't believe in all this nonsense.'

'But what other explanation is there? Think about it, Bimal. A tunnel that not even the birds know about. How can that tunnel get sealed just like that?'

Bimal was worried. 'Yes, that is true.'

'You remember how the smoke was billowing out of this same tunnel yesterday?'

'I remember.'

'And that horrible, clanging laugh?' Bimal was silent at this.

Suddenly Ramhari shouted out, 'Khokababu—look!'

All of us clearly saw a streak of fire zip through the tunnel a few yards ahead.

I came away from the spot where I was standing and started pushing at the rock blocking the entrance with all my strength. It didn't give an inch.

Bimal said, 'Kumar! Light your electric torch and come with me. Ramhari, you bring up the rear. I want to find out what that streak of fire is all about.'

The fire wasn't visible anymore. Bimal walked on, his gun poised to shoot. We followed. My heart was thumping yet again with fear.

A little way ahead, the tunnel had reached another, deeper tunnel. That is where the fire had originally been. We stood there, watchful, looking around us cautiously.

A few yards ahead, something seemed to be lying on the ground. Bagha ran ahead to investigate.

Once the electric torchlight reached the object, Bimal said, 'It looks like a human figure!'

Ramhari asked, 'But why isn't it budging at all?'

Suddenly someone laughed out—hee-hee-hee-hee! We couldn't tell who laughed that terrible laugh and from where it came. We stood, tense and stiff, while the entire tunnel vibrated with the sound of that laughter.

I shrieked. 'Escape, Bimal, escape. Let's run towards the entrance!' But Bimal didn't listen to me. He ran towards the sound instead.

The tunnel fell silent again.

Bimal went right up to the figure lying on the floor, then bent down to touch it, exclaiming almost immediately, 'Kumar, this is a corpse!'

A corpse inside the tunnel? Strange!

Bimal said again, 'Kumar, come here and flash the electric torch on his face, will you?'

I didn't feel like going ahead, but there wasn't much choice in the matter, so I did.

No sooner than I had flashed the torch on the corpse's face that Bimal said, 'Kumar, Kumar—it's Shambhu!'

True enough, it *was* Shambhu. His corpse lay flat on its back, his eyes popped out of his head and there was a gaping wound at his throat!

Bimal bent down again and touched Shambhu, saying, 'There's no hope. He's been dead a long while.'

I removed the torchlight from that horrific scene and asked, 'But—but how did Shambhu get here?'

Struck by this, Bimal said, 'Very true! I hadn't thought of this. How did Shambhu even know about this tunnel?'

I said, 'If Shambhu has come all the way here, then Karali must also know about the tunnel.'

Bimal leapt up. 'Kumar, hold the light steady—the treasure! We have to find where the treasure is first.'

On moving the flashlight all around a few times, we saw a door in one corner of the tunnel.

Bimal ran up to the door, pushed it hard and said, 'Here is a room! The yaksha's treasure must be here.'

# 25

# Invisible Danger

We entered the room and looked all around eagerly. It was a small room, full of dust and stink. All it contained was a stone chest. I had seen a chest like this one at the museum in Calcutta.

Bimal opened the lid of the stone chest. We immediately huddled close to see what was inside, but alas, the chest was completely empty. All our hardship, our effort, our preparation had been in vain! We all fell silent, unable to utter a single word. I felt like wailing out loud.

After a long time, Bimal heaved a sigh and said, 'So we've lost in every way. Neither did we find the yaksha's treasure, nor shall we survive!'

I said, 'Bimal, if only you'd listened to my words of caution earlier. How many times did I tell you: let's go back and forget about the treasure?'

Ramhari said, 'Why are you giving up so quickly? Look around, perhaps it's hidden elsewhere.'

Bimal said, 'Searching any more is just pointless. Can't you see someone's been here before us? Do you think he's returned empty-handed?'

I said, 'This is none other than Karali's handiwork.'

'Hmm.'

'But how did he find out?'

'Very easily. Kumar, we are stupider than the stupidest of donkeys. We were walking on without a care, thinking we'd seen the last of Karali, when *he* was actually following *us*! He must have hidden himself somewhere close by and watched us open the tunnel yesterday. He completed the job last night and sealed the mouth of the tunnel so we couldn't follow him back.'

'But who murdered Shambhu?'

'Karali, of course!'

'But why would he do that?'

'Just in case Shambhu asks for his share of the treasure.'

Abruptly, right above us and all around, that same laugh rang out again: 'Ha-ha-ha-ha-ha!'

I cried out in terror, 'No Bimal, Shambhu was murdered by this…this yaksha!'

Again that same laugh!

Snatching the electric torch from my hands, Bimal ran in the direction of the laugh, Ramhari running close behind him.

I sat alone in that pitch darkness and trembled. Bimal had run off so fast that I was taken completely off guard and couldn't follow him. How dense that darkness was, right in the bowels of the earth! I could feel myself suffocate in its grip. It was impossible to put my terror into words.

Suddenly, I felt someone's warm breath on my back. I tried to call out for Bimal, but no sound came. I tried to escape by moving in front but bumped hard against the wall of the room and fell.

No sooner than I got up again that someone jumped on my back with all his strength, holding me prisoner with arms that were like bands of steel. I tried to free myself, but my assailant flipped me on to my back like a baby. Finding my voice at last, I yelled out as loudly as I could, 'Bimal, Bimal, save me—help!'

My attacker sat on my chest and laughed that terrible laugh. But then in a moment, the laughter turned into a shriek of pain. And with that, the man or ghost, whatever it was that sat on my chest threw itself to the ground.

I sat up quickly. Even though I couldn't see a thing in the dark, I could tell that a violent struggle was going on inside the room.

# 26

## Ghost, Animal, or Human?

Clueless, I sat with my back to the wall, while the sounds of the struggle continued inside the room. Then suddenly, all was quiet.

Bimal had still not returned with the torch, and I didn't dare to get up in the dark. There was no doubt that a terrible struggle was going on inside the room. But for the life of me, I couldn't figure out what it was.

Someone breathed heavily on my neck again. I panicked and jumped back, straining to see in the dark. Two burning eyes were staring at me in the darkness. A few moments lapsed, and the burning eyes steadily crept closer and closer towards me.

I gave up all of hope of living. I crept behind step by step, keeping my eyes fixed on those two burning ones. But I tripped over something all of a sudden and fell with a resounding thud on to the floor, crying out with all my might, sure that this was the end, and realized in a flash that the thing I had fallen flat on my back on was a human being.

There was no time to think about who it was, whether it was alive or dead, where it had come from. Some devil could leap on to my chest again like the last time! Terrified, I glanced up and saw the flash of the electric torch in the tunnel a little distance away. Ah, relief at last!

Courage returned on seeing the light. I hurriedly called out, 'Bimal, Bimal, come quick!'

'What's the matter, Kumar? What happened?' asked Bimal, running as fast as he could towards me, with Ramhari close behind him.

As soon as the light from the electric torch hit the room, I saw Bagha sitting in front of me, panting, his paws outstretched. Fresh blood was smeared all over his face and body. So the eyes that had scared me witless were Bagha's! But why was there blood all over him?

Suddenly Bimal said in a shocked voice, 'Kumar,

what are you sitting on?' Then I realized that there was a human body under me. I leapt up and saw a sight that I shall never forget.

On the floor of the room lay the corpse of a huge, ebony, nearly naked man. The primitive face was almost completely obscured by his long, matted hair and beard. His large eyes stared blankly above and his mouth was open, revealing such big teeth—who *was* he? He looked so odd that it was difficult to tell if he was a monster, a wild animal or a human being.

Bimal bent over for a closer look and said, 'He's bleeding profusely from his throat!'

My own throat felt dry as I spoke.

'Bimal, this man tried to murder me a little while ago.'

'You don't say! And then?'

'I couldn't really say what happened then, as it was pitch dark, but I suspect I'm alive this time round because of Bagha.'

'Because of Bagha?'

'Yes. He's the one who pulled the brute off me by his throat; that's why he's got the wound. But check, is he still alive?'

Bimal checked the body for signs of life and said, 'No, he's dead all right.'

Ramhari patted Bagha on the back and said, 'Shabash, Bagha, shabash.'

Bagha wagged his tail in delight; I pulled him close and hugged him.

Bimal asked, 'But who is this man?'

Ramhari said, 'Ooh—what a terrifying figure he cuts!'

I said, 'I think he's deranged.'

Bimal said, 'Possible. Why would he try to kill you without rhyme or reason otherwise?'

'I think Shambhu probably died at this man's hands.'

Ramhari asked, 'But how on earth did he enter the tunnel in the first place?'

Bimal considered the question in silence. A while later, he said, 'Look, Kumar, we saw some burnt firewood and meat in one corner of the tunnel when we went to investigate who was laughing. From this it is clear to me that this man used to live inside the tunnel. He was the one laughing all along; there isn't a shadow of a doubt in my mind that he was insane.'

I said, 'But the tunnel is sealed!'

Bimal jumped up suddenly at this and said joyfully, 'Kumar, we're saved! We don't have to die in this hellhole any longer!'

I asked, surprised, 'Why are you suddenly so happy?'

Bimal said, 'Kumar, you are a complete idiot. Don't you realize that if that man had made the tunnel his home, then there must be a path leading outside somewhere or the other. The entrance we used, the one as per the message, was always shut. So the man mustn't have used it for his comings and goings. And if he wasn't going out, then how did the meat and the firewood get here?'

I said, 'But even if such a path exists, we don't know how to find it.'

Bimal said, 'Find it, we shall. We have yet to check the entire tunnel.'

'Fine,' I said, 'let's find the path. Now that the yaksha's treasure is out of our reach, let us at least breathe fresh air.'

Bimal said, 'The treasure is not beyond our reach yet. If we find the way out, we can still catch Karali. Come on. Let's not delay any further.'

Bimal led the way, we followed.

We hadn't realized earlier how large the tunnel was, or how many branches it had. We searched every nook and cranny for nearly two hours, but couldn't find the path. All of us felt claustrophobic in that land of ever darkness, but there was no other way out.

Finally, exhausted, I said, 'Bimal, my friend, I can't do this any longer. If the path is never going to be found, let me just lie down and die here,' saying which, I slumped down on the ground.

Bimal held my hand and said softly, as if to a child, 'Kumar, it won't do to give up so easily. There has to be a path and we shall find it at all cost!'

I leaned against the wall of the tunnel and said, 'If you have any stamina left then you go ahead, my body can't take it anymore.'

In the meantime, Bagha stood up all of a sudden, his ears cocked, staring intently at something. Bimal quickly flashed the torch in that direction. We saw a fox standing a little way away, staring at us in silent surprise.

Bagha barked at the fox and chased it. The fox sprang away into the distance in alarm, Bimal's torch following its every move. The fox ran a little further and then jumped up and disappeared. Bagha went up to the spot and stood staring, stumped.

Bimal ran ahead to see how the fox had escaped. He raised the torch above his head and said in delight, 'Kumar, we've found the path!'

Bimal's words gave me a fresh lease of life. I quickly ran up to him and asked, 'Where?'

'There!'

And there it was. Right above us, a small hole, through which came in the silvery haze of morning light. My eyes couldn't get enough of this magical light of our earth's after having been deprived of it for so long.

Bimal said, 'A landslide must have caused this little hole to form. Kumar, you exit first. Ramhari, you hold the torch, let me give Kumar a leg up!'

Bimal lifted me up, I stuck my neck out of the hole and was instantly welcomed by the sun-kissed blue sky, the gentle breeze of the Khasi hills and its flower-filled wilderness like an old friend.

# 27

# Karali's Other Feat

I truly appreciated the beauty of light and fresh air for the first time that day when I emerged from the dark underbelly of the tunnel. No one spoke. We all sat and soaked in the sunlight and the breeze for a while.

Bimal got up with alacrity all of a sudden and said, 'Enough! This breeze and this sunlight will still be there tomorrow. But if we don't catch Karali today, we will never catch him! Kumar, Ramhari, get up!'

I asked from my supine position, 'Where to now?'

'The path we have been walking on, the same one. We'll catch Karali—snatch the yaksha's treasure from him.'

'But we still haven't finished our lunch!'

Bimal yanked me up by the arm and said, 'To hell with lunch! First set out, then we'll rummage in the bag for biscuits. That will do fine while we're walking. Come on, no more dilly-dallying.'

Bimal walked on with the gun on his shoulder, we followed, as always. As he walked, Bimal said, 'Having sealed us in the tunnel, Karali must be thinking he's safe with the treasure now. He's relaxed, he's on his way back home. We'll be able to catch up with him if we just walk faster, perhaps today itself? He couldn't have gone far.'

I said, 'But Karali won't give up the treasure so easily.'

'Of course, he won't.'

'So we'll have another scuffle?'

'Of course, we'll have another scuffle! But this time round, we'll attack him first.'

Chatting like this, we left the Buddhist monastery behind us and walked on. By and by, the sun set, dusk and then darkness fell around us, birds chirped to announce their bedtime, and we reached that big crevasse in the mountain, the one we had to cross by cutting the pine tree and making a bridge. Approaching the bridge, Bimal said, 'You know what I'd have done if I were Karali, Kumar?'

'What?'

'I'd have hurled this tree into that bottomless gap as soon as I crossed. Then no one else would be able to follow me.'

'But Karali knows that his enemies are slowly suffocating to death in the tunnel, that they are powerless to stop him!'

'It is this complacence that will be his undoing and make him lose the treasure. But who's that?'

We all heard perfectly clearly, the faint, imploring voice that tore through the evening air, 'Water... some water!'

'Kumar, whose voice is that?' Bimal asked.

'Water...a little water!'

On searching, we found something like a human body in the gap of the mountain, hidden from plain view in the darkness of the undergrowth. I said, 'Ramhari, quick, light the lantern!'

Once Ramhari lit the lantern and held it over the gap, the man wailed: 'Oh please, please...some water, just a little water!'

He was stuck not very far below, so Bimal yanked him up and said, 'I have seen this man with Karali!'

The man stared at Bimal fearfully and said, 'Please

don't hit me, I'm dying anyway. Hitting me will be of no use to you!'

I noticed at last. Someone had stabbed him repeatedly with a sharp weapon—on his face, his chest, his arms, his back, leaving large bloody scars all over.

Bimal asked, 'Who did this to you?'

'Karali!'

'Karali?'

'Yes, sir, Karali—that devil.'

'But why did he wound you like this?'

'I'll talk, Babu, I'll talk. But first, some water, I beg you… I'm dying of thirst.'

Ramhari quickly poured some water into his open mouth. The man drank a gulpful, said 'aaah' and closed his eyes, staying silent for a while.

Bimal asked, 'Now tell us, why did Karali wound you like this?'

'Babu, I'll tell you everything. I won't make it through the night anyway.'

The man stayed silent for a while longer, then sighed and said, 'Babu, once we had sealed the entrance of the tunnel with the rock, and you inside it, Karalibabu and I left the scene. The box containing the yaksha's treasure was with

Karalibabu. Once we reached this spot, Karalibabu said, "Why don't you cook something? We haven't eaten since lunch yesterday, I'm very hungry." We were carrying rice, dal and potatoes with us. I collected firewood from the jungle, lit a fire and made a khichri. Karalibabu ate a little before I did, then I sat to have my lunch.

'Out of nowhere, there was suddenly a heavy blow on my back, then all went black. As I was losing consciousness, I felt something sharp, like a knife, stab me in the face and chest again and again. I do not know who it was, but there was no one else here except Karalibabu and myself, it couldn't have been anyone else. He must have done it because he didn't want to give me a share of the treasure.' Saying which, the man started panting.

Bimal asked him, 'When did all this happen?'

'It was afternoon then, I think.'

'Who else is there with Karali now?'

'No one. We were five in all. On our way to the monastery, two fell into that gap and died, as you know. We abandoned Shambhu to his fate with that ghost or vampire or whatever that terror was inside. Now it's my turn—water…some water!'

Ramhari poured some water again into his open

mouth. But the man's eyes were bursting out of his head, he could barely gulp.

Bimal leaned forward and asked hurriedly, 'What was in the treasure box?'

But the man could no longer speak. He panted and foamed at the mouth. He hiccupped a couple of times and then was absolutely still.

'Dead,' Bimal said. 'He won't speak again in this lifetime. Come on, let's go, let's catch Karali first.'

Seeing a man die like this in front of my eyes made me feel terrible. I walked on and thought, is there a second scoundrel in this world as heartless as Karali?

# 28

# The Terrible Cave

A feeble moonlight emerged by and by, illuminating nothing but the darkness around us. The barren path—a ghost world—stretched ahead. We seemed to shatter the silence with every footstep. The trees around us, inky in the night, sometimes swayed in the breeze, looking for all the world as if the darkness was beckoning to us.

I told Bimal, 'It wouldn't be right to forge ahead in this dark.'

'Why not?'

'Even Karali must be hesitating to walk alone in this pitch darkness. He is probably resting in a cave somewhere. If we walk on, we'll just leave him behind. Instead, let's rest somewhere for the night, we can always start as soon as it is dawn.'

Bimal said, 'Good idea, Kumar. In my haste to catch Karali, I hadn't considered any of this.'

When the blood-red, hibiscus hued, piercing light of the dawn sun wove a vermillion border across the eastern horizon, we set off again. All around us, birds were chirping their morning song. The leaves on the trees seemed to join in as they murmured along, the waterfalls seemed to leap from rock to rock in the same rhythm. It was all so serene. And there we were—running head on in our lust for violence. The thought filled my mind with guilt. By the time the sun had emerged above hill after hill, we had reached a bend in the road.

Bagha had been leading the way. He suddenly barked out loud when he reached the bend. We were alert enough. Everyone ran to the spot to find out why Bagha was barking.

We saw, some distance away, a man stood staring at us in surprise. Karali! There he was. A big box in his hands—the yaksha's treasure!

Karali made a run for it as soon as he saw us and immediately, Bimal followed suit. The rest of us stood there, dumbstruck.

Bimal had practically caught up with Karali. His voice rang out: 'Karali! If you want to escape with your life, then stop! Otherwise, I shall shoot you dead!'

But Karali didn't stop. He turned abruptly to the left of the path, jumped and disappeared. We saw Bimal stop there, stunned for a moment. Then, he too, turned left and jumped.

Finally, I came to my senses. Shouting 'Ramhari, follow me!', I too ran ahead as fast as I could.

On reaching the spot I saw the mouth of a cave in the hillside. Leaping up immediately to enter, my ears were assaulted by a terrible scream and just after that, another loud scream. It was Bimal's voice this time. Then, all was silent.

My heart shuddered with an unknown fear as I ran inside. When I entered the cave, I found no one there. Nonplussed, I stood still. Ramhari entered the next minute and said, 'Who shouted out like that? Why, where's Khokababu?'

'I don't know, Ramhari. I heard Bimal scream out from inside the cave and rushed in. But now I can't see anyone anywhere.'

One side of the cave was shrouded in misty darkness. Ramhari ran towards it and said, 'Here! There seems to be a path going in.'

Running to the spot, I saw that he was right. A narrow path snaked its way into the cave. But it was all very dark, I could see nothing more.

'Ramhari, take the electric torch out quick, and pass me my gun.'

Ramhari handed me the gun, then took the torch out and entered the path gingerly. I held my gun at the ready and entered with him, casting a cautious eye on our surroundings. Above us, below, on either side was solid stone, walking through this reminded me of the tunnel where the yaksha's treasure was. Suddenly, Ramhari halted in front of me and said, 'Disaster!'

I asked, 'What's the matter?'

Ramhari replied, 'There's a huge hole right in front.'

In the bright light of the electric torch, I saw that the path disappeared right under Ramhari's feet and just after that an enormous, dark emptiness opened its cavernous mouth, waiting to swallow us up! Had Bimal fallen into *that*?

I shouted out as loud as I could, 'Bimal…Bimal… Bimal!'

From the belly of the earth came a feeble, pathetic reply, 'Kumar, Kumar—help! Save me!'

Stretching out at the mouth of that hole, I flashed the torchlight into it. The hole was a good fifty to sixty feet wide. Looking down with the help of the torch, I saw something gleaming roughly thirty feet under. On careful inspection, it turned out to be water.

I shouted out again, 'Bimal, where are you?'

From what seemed like its depths, Bimal's voice replied, 'Here, in the water. Pull me up quickly, Kumar. My arms and legs are cramped. I'm very close to drowning.'

'Ramhari! Quick, take out the bundle of rope from the bag.'

Ramhari sat and opened the knapsack on his back. I flashed the torch downwards and saw Bimal, still swimming in the black waters.

We quickly lowered the rope. Bimal swam across and gripped it with both hands. I shouted again, 'Bimal, don't try to pull yourself up by using the rock face for leverage., We'll pull you up.'

But he replied, 'No. I think I can manage.'

Ramhari and I held tight on to the rope, Bimal climbed up a little later straight into our arms and fainted from exhaustion.

Ramhari and I carried him out into the fresh air.

# 29

# Conclusion

Once Bimal regained consciousness I asked him, 'How did you fall into the cave?'

Bimal said, 'As soon as I entered the cave behind Karali, he skulked into that dark path. I didn't let go either, I followed him in there and grabbed him in that darkness. So began our tussle. But neither of us knew that there was a hole in there. In our jostling around, we grabbed each other and both of us toppled into it.'

I shivered and said, 'What! So Karali's still in there somewhere?'

'Yes. But not alive.'

'What!'

'Although I could barely discern anything in the dark, I can still vouch for the fact that he has drowned. Because I heard a couple of desperate splashes when I fell into the water and then it all went quiet. Karali mustn't have known how to swim, otherwise there would have been more splashes in the water.'

I asked with bated breath, 'And the box containing the treasure?'

Bimal shook his head with a bitter smile. 'He went down with the box, not letting it go even for an instant. I believe he has died with it.'

'But what if the box has fallen somewhere on the path?' I said and snatched the electric torch, entering the cave a second time. But, alas! There was no sign of the box anywhere. I looked searchingly towards that enormous hole. Way down below the lake lay as still and silent as death. Nobody could tell that it had swallowed a man's life and untold treasure so heartlessly just moments ago.

I stepped outside and sat down in a daze; all hope was lost.

Bimal asked, 'What—couldn't find it, could you?'

I shook my head and said, 'No.'

'I knew you wouldn't. Karali has squandered his

life of course, but not the yaksha's treasure. He took the box with him to his death. The final victory is his all right.'

I sat absolutely still. Grief, regret, disgust were filling my thoughts. After all the hardships, all the dangers—*this* disappointment! I felt like crying out loud. Bimal stared listlessly at the ground for a while as well.

After a long while, Ramhari came up and said, 'It won't do to sit around moping like this. So what if the fates hadn't decreed the yaksha's treasure for you? Isn't it enough that you're alive and well? A thing that brought so much danger, so many hassles, took so many lives, god alone knows what harm it would have caused us had it fallen into our hands! Now, head home like good boys while you're both still in one piece.'

Bimal raised his head and laughed at this. 'You're right, Ramhari. Since the grapes are out of reach anyway, let us say they are sour and console ourselves. Can a yaksha's treasure be suitable for human consumption? Let Karali enjoy it for all eternity as a ghost. And let us not bother ourselves about him any longer! But right now, I'm ravenous, Kumar! Try and shoot some pheasants, will you? Ramhari, you cook the rice in the meantime and I'll massage some balm to get rid of my body ache.'

I said, 'And so…'

Bimal completed, 'A long nap after lunch, then to set out for the journey homewards, what say?'

'I guess…'

*Here ends my tale.*